# THE HAUNTED HOTEL

A LIN COFFIN COZY MYSTERY BOOK 13

J. A. WHITING

**Formatting by Signifer Book Design**

**Proofreading by Donna Rich: donnarich@me.com**



**To hear about new books and book sales, please sign up for my mailing list at:**
**www.jawhiting.com**

*For my family with love*

# 1

Lin Coffin startled awake from a disturbing dream and sat up in bed. Her t-shirt was damp from perspiration and her hands felt shaky with the leftover feelings from the nightmare. Her husband Jeff's soft, slow breathing beside her was a comforting sound and she gently placed her hand on his shoulder for a moment.

Her little brown dog Nicky looked up at her from the floor where he was tapping his tail against the wood.

"I'm okay, Nick. It was just a bad dream," she whispered. Lin noticed a bright red light shining into the room from the window facing the road and she thought maybe there had been an accident in front of the house.

She slipped quietly from the bed and patted the dog on his head before going to take a look outside. Pushing the curtain to the side, she glanced up and down the street. There were no police cars and no accident. No one was on the road. No red light shone anywhere outside.

Turning away from the window, Lin narrowed her eyes. The red light was shining into the bedroom. She looked outside again and then back into the room.

*Where is that light coming from?*

She padded softly around the bedroom trying to determine the source of the light, but found nothing. With a sigh, she headed to the kitchen to get a glass of water.

The house was designed in a "U" shape with one wing housing the master bedroom and a bathroom, and with the living room located in the center. A second bedroom that Lin used as an office was off the living space. The other leg of the "U" housed the kitchen and dining area and another bathroom. The living room and kitchen had big windows and doors that led out to the large deck.

With the dog following behind her, she walked through the living room and glanced out to the deck. Moonlight lit up the outside and streamed in through the windows making it seem like a small lamp had been left on in the room.

In the kitchen, she poured a glass of water, and as she was sipping, she turned towards the windows ... and almost dropped her glass.

Red light lit up the deck and shone into the kitchen.

Lin hurried to the door and flung it open.

Nicky whined.

"What's causing this light?" she asked the dog. "Is there a comet or a meteor shower or what?" She stepped onto the deck to gaze up at the sky.

Nicky's tail pounded the deck so vigorously that it caused Lin to shift her eyes to him.

"What's up, Nick?" Lin looked to where the dog was staring, and gasped, as an icy wave of air enveloped her.

A translucent woman stood beyond the deck and patio at the edge of the field behind Lin's house. She wore a long dress and her hair was styled half-up and half-down. An almost blinding red glow streamed out of the woman, lighting up everything around her.

"Oh." Lin squinted from the brightness, but made eye contact with the ethereal woman. They peered at one another for almost a full minute.

The woman's expression was neutral and calm. She didn't appear to be distressed or anxious in any way. She looked at Lin with some familiarity, as if they might have known one another in the not so distant past, but Lin didn't recognize the ghost. She'd never seen a spirit give off light like this one was doing ... and certainly not such a bright red light. On occasion, when a ghost was angry or upset, he or she might flare red just before disappearing, but that was very different from what this particular spirit gave off.

"Are you okay?" Lin asked the spirit.

Nicky whined and wagged his tail like he wanted to run to greet the ghost.

The woman stared at Lin.

"Do we know each other?"

The ghost's expression didn't change.

"Does your red light mean that something is wrong?"

The ghost woman gave an almost imperceptible nod.

"Do you need something from me?"

The word *yes* seemed to form in Lin's mind.

Lin shivered from the chill on the air. "Can you tell me, or show me what you need?"

After several seconds, the woman tilted her head

a little to one side, and then blinding red sparks seemed to fly out from her body. In a moment, a brilliant flash of red lit up the night, and she was gone.

Lin took a long, deep breath while she stared at the spot where the ghost had stood. "Well. We haven't seen anything like that before, have we, Nick?"

The dog woofed.

"Lin?" Jeff stood at the kitchen door rubbing his eyes. "Why are you on the deck? Is something wrong?"

"I had a visitor."

"Oh?" Jeff's eyes widened. "Is the visitor gone?"

"Yes." Lin walked over to the doorway to give her husband a hug. "It was a woman. It was the strangest thing. A bright red light emanated from her. It was like the light was coming out through her pores."

"Was she in pain?" Jeff ran his hand over Lin's long brown hair.

"She didn't seem to be. She seemed calm."

"Come in here. Your skin is like ice." Jeff took her hand. "Want a cup of tea? I'll put the kettle on."

Lin sat at the kitchen counter and told Jeff how she happened to be out on the deck while he put the tea kettle on the stove and gave Nicky a dog treat.

"I had a nightmare and woke up with a start."

"What was the nightmare about?" Jeff took two mugs from the shelf.

Lin rubbed at her forehead. "I don't know. The past few nights, I've woken up from a nightmare, but I can never remember what it was about. All I know is I'm terrified. Someone I care about is in danger. All I can recall is that awful sensation that someone needs me to help them and I can't figure out how to get to them." She shuddered and ran her hands over her arms. "I don't know who it is who needs help and all I can see around me is darkness. I don't know where I am."

Jeff poured the tea and set one mug in front of his wife. "Dreams can be some leftover worry from the day. Maybe it's something about work, maybe something needs to get done, but it's being overlooked."

"That could be, but it feels more serious than that. It's something that feels very dangerous." A wave of anxiety washed over Lin as she tried to sort out her feelings from the dream.

"It'll work itself out." Jeff kissed Lin on the top of the head. "It'll be okay."

Almost nine months ago, Lin and Jeff, and Lin's cousin and best friend, Viv, and her husband, John, were married in the fall in a double wedding ceremony, and celebrated with a reception in the yacht club down by Nantucket harbor. It had been a day full of joy and love, and everyone had a wonderful time. It had been a peaceful and uneventful rest of the fall, winter, and spring with no ghosts needing any assistance ... until now.

"Viv will be glad to hear we have another ghost who needs some help," Lin said.

Jeff laughed. "Oh, yeah, I bet she'll be thrilled."

Viv was never eager to step in when a spirit needed something from them, but she was always by her cousin's side when something had to be figured out or resolved. She herself was able to see the ghost of one of her long-ago relatives, and the ghosts who appeared at her wedding. "Those were things never to be repeated. I hope," Viv had said. "I'll leave seeing ghosts to you," she'd told Lin. "That's your specialty, not mine."

Lin, on the other hand, had been able to see ghosts since before she could remember. When she was in elementary school, she decided she didn't want to see them anymore, and for a long time, she didn't ... until she returned to the island where she was born. And since then, ghosts had been frequent visitors.

"Ready to head back to bed?" Jeff asked. "That alarm is going to go off bright and early."

Lin took his hand, and with Nicky trotting ahead of them, they went to the bedroom, turned off the light, and were soon fast asleep.

An hour later, Lin bolted upright, her heart racing, her palms sweaty, and her mind disoriented.

The dog had been sleeping at the foot of the bed, and he wiggled over the quilt to Lin who wrapped him in a hug.

"That nightmare again, Nick." Lin rocked a little with the dog in her arms. "When is it going to stop?" she whispered not wanting to wake Jeff.

She closed her eyes and took some slow, deep breaths. "I need to remember the dream. Maybe then, it will go away."

All the sensations of the nightmare were readily accessible, but the cause of the terrible feelings was just out of reach. Lin tried to recall any detail she could remember.

Someone desperately needed her, it was a matter of life and death. She had to get to them in time or she would never see them alive again. Tiny glimpses of shadows popped into her mind and she tried to see who she needed to reach and where they were.

Darkness flickered over the blurry images preventing her from making anything out.

She rested back on her pillow and Nicky squeezed in between her and Jeff and snuggled close to her as she patted his head slowly and gently.

With a deep sigh, Lin told the dog, "I need to understand what this nightmare is trying to tell me. I'll figure it out ... I hope." A shiver of worry ran over her skin. "At least there isn't a blazing red light streaming into the room ... for now."

Lin closed her eyes, and Jeff's rhythmic breathing and the warmth of the sweet dog lying next to her lulled her to sleep.

# 2

Lin and her landscaping business partner, Leonard Reed, were removing annuals, perennials, and small bushes from the truck and loading them into two wheelbarrows. Nicky sat supervising the work.

In his sixties, Leonard was tall with muscular shoulders and arms, the result of decades of outdoor labor. A few years ago, he and Lin decided to start their own landscaping business and they'd developed a reputation as the best gardeners and landscape designers on the island. When she'd arrived back on Nantucket after years away and met Leonard for the first time, Lin was certain the man had murdered someone, and when she realized her mistake, she was ashamed of her suspicions that he could be a suspect.

"Oof." Leonard groaned as he took hold of the wheelbarrow handles and started around the side of the large Colonial to the rear yard, with the dog bounding ahead of him.

"What's wrong?" Lin asked with a smile. "Have a tough night?"

"My evening consisted of me making and eating dinner, reading for an hour, and then heading to bed early." When Leonard reached the edge of the new flower bed they'd dug and filled with fresh loam, he stretched his back before reaching for the pots of flowers.

"Where was Heather?"

"She had things to do. We aren't together all the time, you know?"

Leonard had been happily dating a Nantucket lawyer for over a year. In her fifties with shoulder-length, light brown hair, Heather Jenness owned a law firm on the island, did a lot of charity work, and doted on Leonard.

When he reached for a long-handled shovel, Leonard let out a yawn and Lin eyed the man.

"Are you feeling okay?"

"Yeah, I'm fine. I haven't been sleeping well this week." He began to dig a hole in the bed.

"Can't fall asleep?" Lin asked, beginning to feel a little uneasy.

"I fall asleep just fine. I've been having nightmares."

Lin's heart seemed to stop for a few beats. "What sort of nightmares?"

The tall man leaned on the shovel. "I'm in the dark. I can't see anything except shadows and darkness. I'm desperately trying to find someone. Someone I care about is in danger and I have to get to the person, but I can't find the way. I wake up in a cold sweat and have trouble falling back to sleep."

Nicky woofed.

Lin cleared her throat. "How long has this been going on?"

"Four or five nights." When Leonard bent to pick up some flower pots, he noticed the look on Lin's face and he straightened, concern etched in his expression. "What's wrong with you?"

Lin's lower lip trembled and her throat was so dry, she could barely squeeze the words out. "I've been having the same dreams."

Staring at the young woman, Leonard didn't say anything for several moments. "What do you mean?"

"I've been having the same nightmares. Mine are just like yours."

Leonard placed the pots on the ground, wiped his hands on his jeans, and looked Lin in the eyes. "How do you mean?"

Taking in a long breath, Lin stared off across the yard. "I've been having nightmares for four or five nights. In the dream, I'm in the dark, just like you. I'm searching for someone who's in trouble, someone who needs me. I can't find them, just like you can't find the person you're looking for. I wake up in a panic."

Running his hand through his hair, Leonard asked, "What does it mean? How can we both be having the same dreams? Have we been watching something on television or reading the same book that's giving us nightmares?"

"Jeff and I usually work on the second floor renovations after we have dinner. I haven't been watching any television this week."

Leonard looked down at the lawn. "Neither have I."

"I haven't been reading either. If I'm not exhausted at the end of the day, I work on my puzzle books." Lin wiped some perspiration from her forehead.

"I'm reading a biography right now." Leonard's face was scrunched up in thought. "The book has nothing weird or scary in it that would cause nightmares. Is there anything we're both doing this week that might make our minds conjure up a nightmare?"

Lin shrugged. "I can't think of anything."

"Since you can see ghosts and all that, do you have any idea what would make two people have the same dreams?"

"No, and anyway, *you* can see ghosts, too."

"I could only see Marguerite," Leonard corrected his partner. Marguerite was the man's beloved wife who had died years ago in an automobile accident on the mainland. For a long time, Marguerite's ghost inhabited their house and had only crossed over a little more than a year ago.

"I don't know." Lin rubbed at the back of her neck. "I don't know what's going on. I'll talk to Libby. She'll have an idea about what it all means." A lifelong native of Nantucket, Libby Hartnett was a distant cousin of Lin's who had powers of her own and had been an invaluable guide in helping Lin understand her ability to see ghosts.

"Good idea." Leonard looked a little nervous. "Why don't you call her right now."

Lin shook her head. "I think I should wait. It's not an emergency. After work, I'll go to Viv's bookstore. Libby is often there in the late afternoon to get a coffee."

"Okay. Call me after you talk to her. I want to know what this is all about."

"Do you have any idea who is in danger in your dream?" Lin asked.

"None. You?"

"I don't know either. Do you think we're dreaming about the same person?"

"How the heck do I know, Coffin? The whole thing is kind of freaking me out."

Even though it was freaking her out, too, Lin placed her hand on Leonard's arm to reassure him. "We'll figure it out. Maybe it's just some crazy coincidence that we're having the same dreams."

"Nightmares. They're nightmares," Leonard said.

Lin nodded. "I have something else to tell you."

Leonard exhaled loudly. "Now what?"

Lin described the visitor she had last night.

"A bright red light? Why that?"

"I have no idea."

"Did you get a bad feeling from this ghost? Is she going to try to hurt you?"

"That's not the feeling I got. I didn't feel like I was in any danger."

"Red light, huh? What's that about? Just what we need, another weird thing to figure out."

Lin shook her head. "Yeah. Go ahead and add it to the long list of things I don't have a clue about."

Leonard picked up the flower pots he'd set down a few minutes earlier. "We better get to work if we want to finish on time today. We can't stand around wondering what the heck is going on. Let's do something we have control over."

"Good idea." Lin carried the shovel to the bed and began to dig more holes. "Hard work will make us feel less worried."

The man grunted. "I'll let you know at the end of the day if I feel less worried or not." Leonard set the flowers into the hole and gently tamped down the soil around the roots. "I've been thinking recently that you hadn't seen a ghost since the wedding. I was concerned for a while. Glad to see you haven't lost your skills."

Lin chuckled. "Of course, it couldn't be a normal ghost. It has to be one that gives off some mysterious red light."

"Well, you always love a challenge." Leonard moved to the next hole.

"Do I?" Lin's voice sounded slightly weary. "I think you're thinking of someone else."

When they finished up with the first client of the day's gardens, Lin, Leonard, and Nicky headed to three other homes where they took care of the lawn mowing and the yard work.

When it was lunchtime, they spread a blanket under a tree in a nearby park they were driving past. They took their cooler bags from the truck and sat in the shade to eat their lunches. Nicky rested on the blanket with them.

"Let's not talk about the nightmares." Leonard opened a container of chili and took a piece of cornbread from his cooler.

"That's fine with me." Lin bit into her hummus and vegetable sandwich after she'd put out some food and a bowl of water for the dog.

"Does Jeff know you're having bad dreams?"

Lin dabbed her lips with a napkin. "I thought you didn't want to talk about it."

"I don't. Does he know?"

"I told him." Lin nodded. "He said bad dreams are sometimes from some conflict or something from the day that needs addressing."

"Do you have something that needs addressing?" Leonard handed a small piece of cornbread to the dog.

"No. Do you?"

"Not that I know about." He scooped a spoonful of chili from his lunch container.

Lin's phone buzzed with a text and when she saw it, she almost dropped her sandwich.

Leonard picked up on her reaction. "Now what the heck is wrong?"

Lin's eyes were wide when she handed him the phone so he could read the text. "It's from Viv."

Leonard sighed as he accepted the phone and stared down at the screen. In two seconds, his head whipped up. "You've got to be kidding me. Is this some kind of a joke?"

"I wish it was." Lin glanced down again at her cousin's text.

*I'm exhausted. I've been having the worst nightmares every night this week. Are you coming by after work?*

# 3

Located on the cobble-stone main street of the town's center, Viv's popular bookstore-café, Viv's Victus, was busy with customers browsing the book aisles and sitting at the café tables sipping beverages and eating cake, soup, or sandwiches.

When Lin and Nicky arrived at the cozy shop right after work, they found Viv behind the counter in the café section. Viv's gray cat, Queenie, jumped down from the easy chair to greet Lin and her dog friend. The two animals trotted off together while Lin went over to order a coffee and talk to her cousin.

"Hey there." Viv started making Lin's drink without her even having to order.

"Looks busy in here." Lin slid onto a stool.

"Don't get too comfortable. I want to sit at a table to chat." Viv had the coffee ready in a few minutes and the young women headed to a table in the back.

"Is Libby here?" Lin glanced around while carrying her coffee mug.

"She hasn't come in yet, but she'll be here. It's her afternoon habit." When Viv sat down, she let out a sigh. "I haven't had a chance to sit for hours. It's been nonstop today. I'm not complaining though. Busy has been great."

Lin sipped her coffee. "What's this about you having nightmares?"

Viv shook her head. "It's the craziest thing. The past four or five nights I've had nightmares that wake me up. I bolt up in bed with my heart racing and my palms all sweaty. I can barely remember the dreams, but I do know I'm in a dark place ... I can hardly see ... and I'm frantically trying to find someone who needs me ... but I can't find the person. Sometimes I wake up two or three times in the night. It's driving me crazy. Why do you think it's happening?"

Lin took in a long breath and wrapped her hands around the warm mug. "What if I told you Leonard is having the same experience."

Viv narrowed her eyes. "What do you mean?"

"For the past few nights, he's been having the exact same dreams that you're having."

Viv's face was expressionless while she gave Lin's comment some thought, and then a look of disbelief washed over her features. "How can that happen? It can't be the same dream."

"His dreams sound pretty similar to yours."

"What's going on in our lives that's causing us to have nightmares like this? It has to be a coincidence that we're experiencing similar nightmares."

"Well, what if I told you I'm having the same dreams, too?"

Staring at her cousin, Viv leaned back a little in her chair, and then a bit of a smile crossed her lips. "Yeah, right."

When her cousin didn't say anything, but just held eye contact, Viv scowled. "You're kidding, aren't you? Oh, no, you aren't kidding at all. What does it mean? What's going on?"

With a soft voice, Lin said, "I don't have any idea what's going on. My dreams are the same as yours and Leonard's. Someone needs help. I have to get to that person. It's a matter of life and death. Wherever I am, it's so dark I can't even see a few inches in front of me. I'm trying to run, but I'm stumbling and I feel like I might fall. My heart pounds. I wake up and I'm all sweaty."

A worried look showed in Viv's eyes. "This is like a horror book I once read. Is everyone in town having the same dreams?"

"Is John complaining of nightmares?" Lin asked.

"No, he isn't. He's been sleeping just fine. What about Jeff? Is he having them?"

"No, only me." Lin took a drink of her coffee and glanced around the café. "Where's Libby? We need some help."

As if on cue, Libby walked into the café, headed to the counter to order, spotted the cousins sitting at the table and waved. When she had her coffee in hand, she headed over to join the young women.

It was hard to guess Libby's age. Lin and Viv thought she was probably in her early to mid-seventies. Slender and fit, her silver-white hair was cut short and layered, and she had piercing blue eyes. Her family had owned a farm on the island for over a hundred years and she'd grown up in the sprawling mid-island farmhouse. Sometimes, because of her skills, Libby helped a Nantucket detective with some of his cases.

"Why do you two look so glum?" Libby set her purse on the floor.

"We have something unusual to run past you," Lin told her.

Raising an eyebrow a few millimeters, she tilted her head to the side. "What is it?"

Lin gave a summary of what she, Viv, and Leonard had been experiencing and then reported the ghostly visitation by the spirit-woman who gave off bright red light.

Viv's eyes widened at the news of the ghost. "You didn't tell me about that woman." Her tone was almost accusatory.

"I just got here," Lin defended herself. "I didn't have time to tell you before Libby showed up. It's not something that's easy to explain by text. I wanted to tell you in person."

"Is it related?" Viv asked. "Are the nightmares and the ghost woman related?"

With a slightest of shrugs, Lin said, "I'd guess *yes* on that."

"Let's discuss," Libby suggested in her usual no-nonsense way. "I want you each to tell me about your dreams. Vivian, you go first. Don't leave anything out. Tell me the details as you remember them. But before you begin, I want Carolin to leave the table." She turned to Lin. "I don't want your telling of your own dreams to be influenced by what you hear. Go ahead, now. Come back in ten minutes."

Lin got up and walked around the bookstore, and turning into an aisle between the shelves, she spotted Queenie and Nicky asleep on an easy chair tucked away in a corner. She smiled when she saw them, but kept walking so as not to bother their rest. When ten minutes had passed, she returned to the table in the café section.

"Vivian has given her account. Now I'd like to hear your experience," Libby told the young woman.

Lin reported on her own dreams and then explained what Leonard had told her about his nightmares. "And that's about it." The entire time she was telling about her nightmares, Lin rubbed her horseshoe necklace between her thumb and index finger. The necklace was once owned by her ancestor, Emily Witchard Coffin and it was found in her cousin Viv's storage shed, hidden there hundreds of years ago by Emily's husband, Sebastian, an early settler of Nantucket.

In the center of the pendant was a white-gold horseshoe which tilted slightly to one side. The design of the horseshoe could be seen in the chimney bricks of several old houses on the island and was intended to ward off witches and evil spells.

After hearing Lin's account, Libby nodded, looking deep in thought. "Do you know that it's been reported through the ages of people sharing the same dreams? It's called mutual or shared dreams. Imaginal realms are simply different aspects of reality. People can visit a time or place together in their dreams and can do so at the same time. People have also discovered things about a probable future through dreaming, and have learned things about the past as well. Some people have a holographic element to their dreams, or are actually experiencing a different frequency or dimension."

"What do you mean?" Viv asked with a look of distaste, "like time travel or something?"

"Not exactly. It's more like the mind is traveling while dreaming."

"I don't get it." Viv groaned and pressed a finger to her temple. "Why would anyone do that? Shouldn't the person have to give permission to dream the same dream as someone else?"

Libby kept a smile from forming. "It's a new experience for you. Give yourself time to embrace it."

"Oh, no way." Viv shook her head. "I want it to stop. Right now. I do not give myself permission to share in this dream thing." She looked at Libby. "Can I say that?"

Libby said, "You can say anything you'd like, however, you may continue to have these dreams despite your reticence. I suggest you embrace them and allow them to tell you their story."

"Why?" Lin leaned forward. "What would be the reason?"

Libby glanced from Lin to Viv. "Because someone needs your help, and it might be best to figure out who, where, and when ... so you'll be ready."

"Do you think my new ghost has some connection to these dreams?" Lin questioned.

"Most definitely."

"Oh man," Viv moaned.

"Vivian, you have the ability to see and assist spirit-people," Libby pointed out. "I know you don't want to see them, and I know that you've only been able to see one ghost. But you have a skill and it might be worthwhile to cultivate that skill for the benefit of others."

Viv pouted. "But Lin can help them and I help Lin. It works for us. I don't want a bigger role."

"Maybe someday," Libby whispered as she turned and made eye contact with Lin. "When you enter one of these dream states, try to remove yourself from the emotion of it. Distance yourself from what's happening. Try to analyze the details of the event. Be open to little clues that give you an idea of where you are, of who you are trying to reach." Libby turned her focus to Viv for a moment. "And pay attention to what's keeping you from reaching the person who needs you."

"Okay. We can try to do that," Lin said.

Viv looked appalled by her cousin's agreement. "How do we do that when we're in the middle of a dream?"

Libby said calmly, "Tell yourself that you are in a dream. Try to breathe slowly. When your fear and nervousness lessen, try to figure out what is going on. It may take several attempts to manage your emotions, but eventually you will succeed."

"That makes sense," Lin nodded.

"Does it?" Viv looked like she thought her companions were crazy.

"Vivian," Libby said slowly, "you have been through many experiences that the *average* person would consider impossible, yet you know they're real and indeed possible. This is just another one of those experiences you may add to the list."

Lin gave her cousin a grin.

"After you have one of these nightmares, you should get together to discuss them," Libby went on. "Pay close attention to new or repeated details. In time, you will figure out what the dreams are trying to tell you."

"Are any of us in danger?" Viv asked with a shaky voice.

"You aren't in danger while you dream, if that's what you mean."

"That's good to know, but are the three of us who are dreaming these dreams in some sort of real-life danger?"

Libby didn't answer right away, and when she did, she took a deep breath before saying, "Only time will tell."

# 4

Lin and Viv, along with Nicky and Queenie, walked through the neighborhood just outside of town to Viv's pretty Cape style house surrounded by a white picket fence with climbing roses tumbling over it.

"I almost fell out of my chair when Libby told us she didn't know if we were in danger or not." Viv carried a pastry box filled with slices of cakes and an assortment of cookies from the bookstore café.

"She doesn't know if we're in danger," Lin said. "We don't know what the dreams are trying to tell us. She gave us good advice about what to do when we're dreaming. We have to practice staying calm when we're in the midst of the nightmare. We have to remind ourselves that it's only a dream. That way, we can try to understand what's going on. We can look for clues."

"You make it sound so rational." Viv unlocked the front door and swung it open so the cat and dog could rush inside. "I'm not cut out for this stuff. I get too anxious."

"I think you'll be able to analyze the dreams and come up with ideas about why we're having them ... once we get accustomed to looking at them in a non-emotional way."

"I think that's going to take a lot of practice."

The cousins walked through the living room and dining room and into the kitchen where Viv slid open the sliding glass door to the deck.

"Wait until Leonard hears that we have to become investigators in our own dreams." Viv shook her head.

"Oh." Lin pulled out her phone. "Leonard wanted me to call him as soon as I talked to you and Libby." She stepped outside with Nicky and Queenie and while the animals ran down the steps to the yard, Lin made the call. In ten minutes, she was back in the kitchen.

"What did he say?" Viv was removing pots and pans from the cabinets.

"He took it fairly well."

Viv turned around with a smile on her face. "He did not."

"Well, he kind of did." Lin began to cut the peppers in half and scoop out the seeds to prepare stuffed peppers for dinner. "He thinks the whole thing is unbelievable, but on the other hand, he knows there's more to the universe than what meets the eye. He'd rather not be involved, but *it is what it is* he told me. We'll go with the flow."

"How is Leonard so rational and accepting?" Viv started the rice.

Lin shrugged. "Is John going to be home for dinner?"

"No, he's going to his boat after work. I'll meet him there later." Viv's husband, John, had a sailboat moored at the docks in Nantucket harbor. Viv often kidded that he loved the boat more than he loved her. Even though they'd been married for months, John still spent most nights on the boat while Viv stayed at her antique house. The couple had been together for over ten years before getting married and their arrangement suited them just fine.

"Jeff's working late so he won't be joining us for dinner," Lin said.

"Bring some stuffed peppers home to him," Viv suggested. "I'll bring John some of the leftovers when I go down to the boat later."

While the meal was baking, the cousins took glasses of wine, a bowl of nuts, and a plate of crackers and cheese out to the table on the deck. Queenie and Nicky rested in the grass watching birds and squirrels in the trees.

"So tell me more about the new ghost." Viv placed some cheese on a cracker. "Do you have any ideas about why she's all lit up in red?"

"I don't. When ghosts give off red flares or sparkles, it usually indicates anger, but this spirit doesn't seem that way at all. She just looks at me like she wants to ask me something. Her expression is one of someone who needs help, not of someone who is full of anger or rage."

"Well, that's a plus." Viv looked out over the backyard's green lawn and then looked back to Lin when a thought popped into her head. "Oh. Do you think this ghost is the person we're all looking for in our dreams?"

Lin thought over the possibility. "That's an interesting suggestion. Maybe she'll use the dreams to tell us what she needs from us. When we dream, we should try to remember that she might be the one we're trying to rescue."

"What did she look like?"

"She had on a long dress. Her hair was in a half-up, half-down style. I couldn't tell what color hair she had. She was very faint and transparent. She seemed to be a little older than us ... maybe in her forties. She wasn't wearing any noticeable jewelry, but I was more focused on the red light that was streaming from her. You know how sometimes you get a feeling about someone's personality when you first meet? I thought this ghost seemed like she was a nice person."

"That's a good thing." Viv sipped from her wine glass. "Maybe she isn't out to kill us or anything."

Lin chuckled. "If she wants our help with something, then murder better not be on her mind."

"I'm a little afraid to go to sleep tonight," Viv admitted.

"I know. We have to keep repeating that it's a dream, not real life. We need to focus on understanding the message that's trying to be sent to us."

"Yeah, right. Don't be surprised if I call you in the middle of the night for a pep talk."

"Maybe you should call Leonard," Lin told her with a grin. "He's a lot more empathetic than I am."

"I'll keep that in mind."

After dinner, Lin and Nicky headed home, and she was happy to see Jeff's truck in the driveway. When she opened the door, she said, "I'm back."

"I'm upstairs," Jeff called. He leaned over the second floor balcony that looked down to the living room. "I thought I'd get started." He took in a deep breath. "What smells good?"

"Stuffed peppers. And a slice of chocolate cake from Viv's café."

Jeff's eyes widened. "I'll be right down."

Nicky ran to greet the man and was rewarded with some playful pats.

Lin sat at the kitchen island with Jeff, and while he ate, she told him what she'd learned from Libby.

"Oddly, it makes sense," Jeff admitted. "I remember reading an article about shared dreams. At the time I thought it was cool, but I didn't really believe it could be possible. Live and learn, I guess. I've come to understand that there are far more possibilities in the world than I ever imagined." He leaned over and kissed Lin. "Thanks to you."

After Jeff finished eating, he rinsed his plate and

utensils and slipped them into the dishwasher. "Ready to do some work?"

"Nope." Lin laughed. "But I know we have to." She and Jeff went up to the second floor where they were going to renovate the empty attic space to add two more bedrooms, an office for Jeff, a sitting space, and two bathrooms.

Jeff had sold his house on the other side of the island right after the wedding and moved into Lin's cottage. A carpenter, handyman, and renovator, Jeff was skilled and experienced, but doing the second floor renovation work themselves after long days at their jobs was not ideal. It would take a lot longer to manage the renovation by doing it on their own. They decided that they wouldn't try to rush or put pressure on themselves to make the changes quickly.

They'd already cleaned out the space of boxes, books, and other items left behind by Lin's grandfather who had lived in the house for decades. An electrician had wired the space for electricity, the old insulation was removed and replaced, and the subfloor was redone, and now, drywall was being installed, working from the space over the master bedroom to the new sitting area over the living room, to the section of the house over the kitchen.

Lin had just picked up the nail gun when Jeff

told her, “I found another box over in that corner.” He gestured. “There was another small closet tucked under the eaves.”

“Okay.” Lin took a step towards her husband to help put the sheetrock panel in place and then she stopped. A flutter of unease washed through her veins and she turned to look in the direction where Jeff had indicated the box had been placed.

“Did you look in the box?”

“I took a quick look. There are some old pamphlets, magazines, things like that.” Jeff measured a section of the wall.

Lin turned around towards her husband, but something pulled her in the opposite direction.

“Do you mind if I take a peek at the box?” She glanced over her shoulder.

“Sure, go ahead.” Jeff busied himself with taking more measurements.

Walking slowly to the box, Lin stared down at it, then sat on the floor, and opened the lid. She took out some of the pamphlets her grandfather had saved and flipped through them. There was a small paperback book put together decades ago by the island historical society and inside there were old photographs of buildings and homes of Nantucket along with a few paragraphs of history on each one.

Placing it on her lap, the pages fell open to the middle of the booklet ... and Lin's eyes widened. At her favorite beach, Surfside, stood a grand old hotel. Looking at it caused a rush of anxiety mixed with a strange sense of despair ... and longing.

"Did you know there was once a hotel on Surfside beach?" she asked her husband.

"A hotel?" Jeff came over to have a look. "I think I remember seeing that picture in an old book. I don't know anything about it."

They stared at two pictures on the middle pages. One showed the hotel in its heyday looking new and inviting. A large wraparound porch encircled three sides and rocking chairs and lounge chairs were placed around it. The second photo showed the collapsed hotel looking sad and forlorn.

"There was a fire in it. It was a total loss," Lin read the short paragraph. "It had to be knocked down."

"Too bad. It looked like a really nice place." Jeff went back to his work.

Lin closed the booklet and stood, holding it tightly in her hand. It was nearly dark outside, and as she turned to head over to help Jeff, a flickering of red light streamed through the window.

Taking a look outside as she passed by, she saw someone standing in front of the house.

The ghost-woman stared in the window, her eyes locked onto Lin.

# 5

When Lin and Leonard arrived at Anton Wilson's antique home to mow the lawn and tend to the landscaping, the historian, wearing an apron, flung open the door and waved them over.

"I made breakfast. Come in and eat. I won't take no for an answer." In his early seventies, Anton, a thin and wiry man with intelligent eyes, was a retired professor, author, and expert on Nantucket's past.

Lin, Leonard, and Nicky went inside to Anton's large, cozy kitchen that had a large hearth on one wall and a long wooden table set in front of the fireplace.

"I was in the mood to cook." Anton had already

set the table and in the center was a vase of spring flowers next to a plate of sliced banana bread, a bowl of sliced strawberries, blueberries, and raspberries, a pot of coffee, and a pitcher of freshly-squeezed orange juice.

"I hope you're hungry." The man brought a platter of pancakes and sausages to the table. "Go ahead now. Don't let it get cold. Come here, Nicky, I have some leftover chicken from last night for you." He scooped pieces of chicken into the dish he kept in the kitchen for the dog.

"It sure smells good." Leonard took a seat and didn't wait to be told again. He dug in and filled his plate.

Suddenly, Anton stopped what he was doing and stared at Lin. "What's wrong with you?"

Lin sat and poured herself a cup of coffee. "Why do you ask that?"

"Because I've known you for a long time and I can tell when something is on your mind."

"Spill it, Coffin," Leonard encouraged in between bites.

"I knew it." Anton took the seat next to Lin. "It's a new ghost?"

"Well, yes, but there's something more."

The historian's eyes narrowed and bored into the young woman sitting beside him.

"Have you talked to Libby recently?" Lin asked.

"I spoke with her the day before yesterday, but she didn't share anything about a new incident." Anton was practically bursting with curiosity, but he reined it in to give Lin time to speak when she was ready.

After lifting a pancake from the serving platter to her plate, Lin reached for the maple syrup before giving Anton the story of the shared dreams and the ghost-woman who gave off the red light.

"Fascinating. Shared dreams. I've heard of that phenomenon, but I haven't known anyone who had experienced such a thing." Anton looked from Lin to Leonard as if he were examining two specimens.

"Well." Lin wiped her lips with her napkin. "Now, you know three people who have."

Anton asked questions of his guests and they answered what they could.

"Libby said that when we're experiencing the nightmare, we need to remind ourselves that we're in a dream and try and stay calm and not get wrapped up in it."

Leonard scoffed. "Easy for her to say, not easy for me to do."

"Me either," Lin admitted. "Libby also told us to watch for repeated details in the dreams. Those details could be clues to the meaning of the nightmares."

"This is very exciting." Anton's eyes sparkled with interest.

"Maybe I'll try to transfer my dreams over to you." Leonard took two more pancakes from the platter and added a scoopful of berries to his plate. "Since you have more appreciation for them than I do."

"I would love that." The historian looked wistful.

"Something happened last evening while Jeff and I were working on the second floor renovation that I wanted to talk to you about," Lin addressed Anton.

Leonard's eyebrows went up. "You didn't tell me about that."

"I wanted to wait and tell both of you at the same time," Lin explained. She told the men about finding the booklet published by the historical society in a small closet put there by her grandfather. "The booklet had pictures and descriptions of places around the island, homes, buildings, boats. I found something interesting inside. There was a picture of a hotel that used to be at Surfside."

"I know the hotel you mean." Anton nodded. "The Surf Hotel. A section of it burned and later, the whole thing was knocked down. What piqued your interest about it?"

"When I was looking at the old photograph, a strange feeling came over me." Lin almost shuddered recalling the sensation that had flooded her body.

"What sort of a feeling was it?" Leonard asked his partner.

"I felt anxiety. I felt desperation." Lin cleared her throat. "I felt a yearning for something that was about to be lost."

Anton and Leonard sat in silence, their eyes pinned on the young woman.

"Those feelings must have some connection to our dreams," Leonard suggested.

Lin nodded.

Anton said, "So that old hotel is wrapped up in this mess."

"Yes," Lin said in a soft voice. "I think it is."

"And to the new ghost," Leonard concluded.

"I saw her last night."

Leonard's eyes went wide. "Where?"

"After I looked at the booklet, I stood up to go back to working on the renovation. She was outside

... in front of the house. I saw her from the second floor window. She was looking up at me."

"Was she giving off her weird red light?" Leonard asked.

"Yes."

"Okay, so we've got our dreams, the old hotel, and this ghost-woman," Leonard summarized. "Now what's it all mean? What does she want from you? What does she want from *us*?"

Lin turned to Anton. "Do you know any more about the Surf Hotel? Do you know what caused the fire?"

Anton pushed his black-rimmed eyeglasses up to the bridge of his nose. "I don't know a whole lot about the place, but I do recall that it was assembled in the 1880s."

"Why do you say assembled?"

"I'll get to that in a minute," the historian said hurrying to his office. When he returned to the kitchen he was carrying a book. He flipped through the pages. "Here we are. A railroad train ran around the island from 1881 to 1917 and provided access to the Surfside area. Like they are now, the views were beautiful and there were pleasant breezes off the ocean. It was decided that a hotel was needed at

Surfside so a developer had a Rhode Island hotel disassembled and brought over to the island on a barge. It was reassembled at Surfside between 1882 and 1884. It was five stories tall, had a wraparound porch, and there was a piazza in the back where band concerts were held. It was a fine, stately hotel."

"Then the fire hit?" Leonard asked.

Anton held up his index finger as he summarized more from the book. "Hold on. Winter storms caused terrible erosion and the dunes receded dramatically and soon the steps to the hotel were a mere couple hundred feet from the edge of the dunes. The railroad decided to close the Surfside section of the train and that spelled doom for the hotel. It's important to note that at that time, automobiles weren't allowed on Nantucket roads so there was no sensible way to transport visitors to the hotel."

"Did the hotel close then?" Lin asked. "Did it go out of business at that time?"

Anton shut the book. "I remember that the hotel was sold at auction in 1896. Someone from Boston bought the place. By then, it was not in pristine condition. I don't recall when it officially closed to visitors. In 1899, the building collapsed. Someone else bought it in 1901. It was cleared away and the land was returned to the town."

"When was the fire?" Leonard questioned.

"I believe the fire happened sometime after it was sold at auction, but I might have the dates mixed up."

"Was anyone killed in the fire?" Lin asked.

"I'm not sure. I can look into that later this afternoon," Anton said.

Lin refilled her coffee mug. "So my ghost-woman must have some connection to the hotel either as a tourist who visited the place, someone who was impacted by the fire, or who knew someone who had an association with the hotel."

"What about our dreams?" Leonard asked. "Why are we having them? Where are we in the dream? Who are we trying to save? And what are we trying to save the person from?" He reached down to pat the dog who was sitting at his feet. "And why are the three of us having the nightmares? Isn't one person enough?"

Lin lifted her hands in a helpless gesture. "I don't know the answers to any of that."

"All of this hasn't even been going on for a week," Anton pointed out. "The investigation is at the earliest stage. Clues will be revealed and details will fall into place." The historian looked to Lin. "You have not yet been stymied by a ghostly mystery."

With a groan, Lin said, "There's always a first time."

"No, in this case, there isn't." Anton looked sure of his statement.

"I wish I could be as positive as you are."

"Believe in yourself, Carolin. The way we all believe in you."

Nicky yipped in agreement.

Lin's eyes got moist from Anton's comments and she rubbed at her lids for a moment. "We'd better get going on the yard or we'll be working until midnight. Thank you for the breakfast."

"You're very welcome." Anton wrapped up some banana bread for the two landscapers to take with them. "I'll spend some time doing a bit of research into the hotel. I'll let you know what I discover."

When they were outside working in the flower beds, Lin asked, "Did anything stand out in your dreams last night?"

Leonard put some flats of flowers down next to the bed. "I got a weird feeling when I woke up from the third and last nightmare of the night."

"What sort of weird feeling?" Lin pulled a few

weeds from between some of the flowers and tossed them in a bucket.

"I don't know why, but I've been thinking." Leonard rubbed at the back of his neck. "In these dreams, maybe we're not searching for someone ... maybe we're searching for *something*."

# 6

After they got home from work, Lin and Jeff took a bike ride around the island using the miles of bike paths that ran by marshes, beaches, woods, and meadows. It was a beautiful early evening with warm temperatures, a cooling breeze here and there along the route, and a lovely blue sky overhead. Stopping to take a drink from their water containers, Lin and Jeff stood off the path in the shade of some trees. Lin had told her husband what was discussed that morning at Anton's house and Jeff was especially interested in Leonard's theory that they might not be trying to find a person, but instead, a thing.

"My first thought when he told us his idea was acceptance," Lin said. "I didn't discount it as being wrong ... which surprised me. Leonard might be on the right track. We have to keep an open mind about it and keep it as an option."

"I agree with you. Until more is understood, it's best to keep all options open," Jeff agreed. As he took off his bike helmet and pushed at his sweaty hair to move it off his forehead, his phone vibrated in his bicycle bag. "It's Kurt." Jeff read the message and looked over at Lin.

"Is everything okay?"

"Today at work, Kurt told me about an idea he had. He wanted to give it more thought before he made a formal offer to me."

With a curious expression, Lin tilted her head to the side. "What's it about?"

"He wants to take me on as a partner in his construction and renovation business."

A smile spread over Lin's face. "That's wonderful." Then she paused. "It is, isn't it?"

Jeff grinned. "It's a great offer. But we have to consider a few things. Kurt wants to expand the business and he considered a few people before deciding to ask me to go in with him. The new partner will have to commit some money to the business, but will receive fifty-percent of all profits going forward. The cost of our health care would be part of the deal."

"That would be a huge savings for us." Lin looked excited. Since she and Jeff were self-employed, they had to pay for health costs on their own.

"Kurt would form a new business entity adding my name to the company name. I'd have responsibility for speaking with clients, doing some design work, doing some of the business's paperwork. Things like that."

"Well, when you're not working for Kurt, you do all that stuff anyway for your own clients," Lin pointed out. She searched her husband's face. "Do you like the idea of owning a business with Kurt?"

"It appeals to me, yeah. Together we could handle more business and expand beyond what we're capable of doing on our own. We could expand to Martha's Vineyard and to Cape Cod eventually. It might mean time away from home sometimes though."

"Are you okay with that?" Lin asked.

"Are you?"

"I think so. How much time away would it be?"

"Maybe a couple of days every two weeks," Jeff said.

"I think that's okay. We're both pretty stable and

secure. We waited until our thirties to get married. I think we'd be able to handle time apart just fine."

"I think so, too."

"Then it seems like you should accept?"

"One thing concerns me."

"Tell me," Lin encouraged.

"It's a fairly substantial investment for us to make for me to join Kurt. The money will be used to hire more workers and provide the supplies we'll need, in addition to paying a lawyer to draw up the paperwork for the new business."

"How much will it cost?"

When Jeff told her, Lin's breath caught in her throat for a second.

Jeff said, "What if the economy takes a turn for the worst and people hold off on doing renovations and new construction? We could lose our investment."

Lin considered what he'd just said. The thought of losing that much money was frightening to her.

"You're hesitating."

"I'm thinking it over. It's a big sum."

"It sure is," Jeff nodded.

Lin looked at him. "But I think you should do it."

"Really?" Surprise washed over the man's face.

"Yeah. You sold your house recently and made a profit from that. We're using some for the renovation on our house, but there's still money left over. And anyway, we don't have to finish the renovations quickly. We can take our time with it. We have plenty of room in the house as it is. You should take over the space I use for my office. You need it more than I do. I can do my paperwork and my part-time programming work in the kitchen. Or we'll put a small desk in the living room for me. If we lose the money, well, I think it's a chance worth taking. Let's make this work."

A broad smile spread over Jeff's face as he wrapped Lin in a hug. "I'm really excited about this. I didn't want to show how excited I am in case you didn't like the idea."

Lin chuckled. "If it's ever something you want, I don't think you'd have a hard time convincing me to go along with it."

"Thank you," Jeff said.

Lin put her hand gently against his cheek. "You don't need to thank me. We're partners. We support each other. And anyway, if we lose everything, we can always move in with Viv. She has plenty of room."

Jeff's laugh was hearty and warm as he hugged

Lin again, then they clinked their water containers together for good luck.

"To new beginnings," Lin toasted.

Jeff chuckled as he said, "To *profitable* new beginnings."

They got back on their bikes and continued on their ride, eventually ending up at Surfside beach. They pulled into the small parking lot and locked their bikes on the rack before walking over to the dunes to look out over the green grasses and white sand beach to the waves crashing against the shore. There were a good number of people swimming and jumping in the waves and sunning themselves on the beach.

"The waves are huge today," Lin observed.

"I'd love to jump in there and cool off. We should have brought our swimsuits."

"Next time." Lin looked around the dunes and at the land spreading back along the hill. "I wonder where the hotel used to be."

Jeff followed her gaze, and then looked around in that direction. "Maybe down that way?"

"Anton is going to do some research on the hotel this afternoon. I bet he'll find out where it was located." Lin noticed a few sparkles in her vision like she got sometimes before a migraine hit. She blinked a few times, and then slipped on her sunglasses to help against the brightness. "Want something from the snack bar? I might get an iced tea. I feel a migraine might be coming on and the caffeine can help keep it at bay."

They each got iced teas, then took off their shoes, left them with the bikes, and walked down to the beach to sit on the sand near the water before heading home for dinner.

Jeff asked, "Do you have any ideas what the thing could be that the three of you are searching for in your nightmares?"

"I don't know what it could be. What's so important that dreaming about it causes us such anxiety and fear?" Lin rested back on the sand. "We need more historical information about the hotel."

"And how is the ghost-woman connected? Was she a visitor? A tourist? An island resident with some link to the hotel or maybe to the land it was built on?"

"That's an interesting idea."

"I didn't ask you this morning ... did you dream the usual dream last night?" Jeff asked.

"I did. I'm getting better at being less affected by the dream. I'm not as anxious or filled with fear when it happens. Those strong emotions tug at the edge of my mind, but I repeat to myself that it's only a dream and I try to watch it like I'm watching a movie."

"Are you picking up on anything new by being able to control your emotions?"

Lin sat up and watched the people in the ocean. The brightness still hurt her eyes even though she was wearing her sunglasses. "I think the darkness is receding at times. I'm hoping I might be able to make some things out as I move through the dream. Maybe eventually, I'll be able to recognize where I am. Want to head home? The caffeine doesn't seem to be working."

"Let's go then." Jeff stood and held his hand out to Lin to help her to her feet, and then they walked through the sand and up the hill to the parking lot.

On the way up the path, Lin's vision got blurry and watery and she had to stop for a few seconds.

"Shall I ride home and get the truck? You can wait here and rest until I get back. It won't take very long."

"No, I don't think so. It doesn't really feel like a migraine. It feels ... different somehow."

Jeff gave her a look trying to understand what she meant. "How does it feel different?"

Just as Lin was about to try and explain what she

was experiencing, she looked to the left and saw something strange.

The particles in the air were shimmering and shining and they began to gather together, swirling around and around. It looked the way things appear right before a ghost showed up, but this conglomeration of atoms was way too large to be a spirit about to form.

Lin squinted, watching the atoms as they picked up speed. The motion almost made her head spin.

And then, what was attempting to form appeared to her, and what she saw made her heart race and a chill run down her back.

There on the hill, translucent and sparkling in the sunshine, was the Surf Hotel.

# 7

"Jeff. Look over there." Lin pointed.

"What is it? What am I looking for?" Jeff glanced in the direction Lin had gestured.

"There's something on the hill." Lin closed her eyes for a few seconds and gave her head a slight shake, and when she looked again, the hotel was still there, but beginning to fade. "The hotel. The Surf Hotel. It's there, above the dunes."

Jeff's face registered surprise as he turned his eyes from Lin to the sandy hill. "Is it? You can see it?"

"It's going away now."

As the hotel disappeared from view, Lin sank down onto the sand and sat. "Oh, gosh." She rubbed both of her temples. "It was there, as plain as day."

Sitting next to his wife, Jeff asked. “What did it look like?”

“It looked just like the picture in the booklet my grandfather saved.” Lin took in a deep breath. “I’ve never seen a ghost-building before. It took me by surprise.”

With concern, Jeff took Lin’s hand. “Are you feeling okay? How’s your head? Is it worse?”

“It’s getting better. The pain and pressure I felt is going away. It must have been a reaction to the hotel trying to form.” She glanced over her shoulder at the spot where the hotel had stood, and then she smiled weakly at Jeff. “Well, now I don’t have to wonder where the building used to be.”

Jeff smiled. “Are you sure you’re okay?”

“Just feeling a little woozy like all my energy was sapped.”

“Did you see the ghost-woman?”

Lin shook her head and then made a face. “Ouch. My head still feels weird. Let’s go back to the bikes and I’ll sip some water before we ride home.”

Jeff helped her up and they walked up the hill to the parking area where Lin sat and had some water while she rested. In a few minutes, she felt much better and they rode slowly back to the house.

Arriving at home, Nicky was sitting in the

entryway and whined and fussed at Lin when she came inside. His little tail wagged so fast it blurred and he wiggled and gave her leg a lick.

"I'm okay, Nick. Don't worry. I'm fine now." She bent and patted the dog to reassure him.

"This dog senses everything." Jeff gave Nicky an admiring look as he scratched the brown dog behind the ears.

While Lin showered, Jeff warmed up some leftovers and they sat at the table on the deck, eating and watching the setting sun paint the sky with different shades of pink and lavender.

"What did the hotel look like?" Jeff asked as he used the serving spoon to scoop some roasted potatoes onto his plate. "Was it in good shape or was it in a state of disrepair?"

"It looked really nice, like a fine hotel. It gave me the impression that it was well-tended and cared for." Seeing the vision of the hotel at the beach had left Lin with a hearty appetite and after finishing her plate of food, she reached for seconds. "Seeing hallucinations makes me hungry," she kidded.

"Okay. So your vision of the hotel was of the building prior to the fire and its subsequent demise."

Lin gave a nod as she brought a forkful of vegetable shepherd's pie to her mouth.

"But the ghost-woman didn't appear when you saw the hotel?"

"She didn't."

"So are the two connected or not?"

"I would say they are connected." Lin took a long swallow from her water glass. "If they're not connected, then that means I have two mysteries to solve which I hope isn't the case. I need to focus my energies on one at a time."

"Wait until Viv, Leonard, and Anton hear about today's ghostly appearance." Jeff grinned. "I can't wait to see their faces when you tell them about it."

The doorbell rang fifteen minutes later and Viv came through the living room and out to the deck carrying a dessert platter of brownies, chocolate espresso bars, and lemon squares dusted with powdered sugar. "I made these bars yesterday for the café and made extra for our meeting tonight." She sat next to Jeff at the table. "I'm still having these darned dreams so don't mind me if I fall asleep while sitting here."

"Are you still waking up in terror?" Jeff asked. "Or are you able to manage your emotions when the nightmares are going on?"

"I'm getting better at being able to observe what's happening without reacting strongly to it so I'm making progress." Viv took a lemon square from the platter.

"It's very hard not to get involved in the dreams," Lin pointed out as she brought out coffees for everyone. "It takes practice to remove yourself a little so you can watch without getting caught up in the whole thing."

Leonard was next to arrive, carrying a six-pack of craft beer. Nicky ran into the house through his doggy door to meet him and led the man out to the deck where he took a seat next to Lin. "Anton isn't here yet?"

"He texted," Lin reported. "He'll be a few minutes late."

Viv added cream to her coffee and sipped. "Last night, something new showed up in my dreams."

Lin's expression showed apprehension as she waited for her cousin to tell them what she'd experienced.

"It started like always. I'm in a dark place and I'm frantically trying to find someone. I'm trying to run, but my feet feel like granite blocks. I can't make much progress. Then right before I woke up, I saw something in the distance."

"What was it?" Leonard looked like he really didn't want to know.

"It was blurry as if I was looking through heavy fog. For a moment, it cleared a little. I saw a building. It was a fancy old hotel set back a little bit from the dunes. Then it was gone and I woke up."

Lin and Jeff exchanged glances.

Leonard cleared his throat. "I dreamt the same thing last night."

Lin turned her head to stare at her friend. "You didn't tell me that when we were working today."

"I wasn't sure if it mattered. I thought maybe it wasn't connected to the nightmares and just slipped in there as I was waking up. I figured we'd talk about it tonight when we all got together."

Lin shared what happened when she and Jeff were at Surfside beach a few hours ago.

Viv's eyes went as wide as saucers. "Oh, gee. Right on the dunes? Oh, gosh. You've never seen a building before. I mean a building that doesn't exist anymore. Wow. I think I would have fainted. In fact, I'm sure I would have." She made eye contact with Lin. "Thank heavens you're the one who sees these things and not me. Seeing things in my dreams is good enough, thank you very much."

Anton came hurrying around the corner carrying his briefcase. "Sorry I'm late. What have I missed?"

The group filled in the historian on the latest news.

"Well." Anton blinked at the people sitting around the table. "Good, good. Things are progressing. There is definitely a link between the old hotel and the new ghost." Opening his briefcase, he removed his laptop. "My research isn't complete, but so far, I was able to find out a few things." He peered at the screen. "There were three fatalities as a result of the hotel fire. Two women and a man. One woman was a guest at the hotel, the man might have been visiting someone there because authorities couldn't determine if he was a registered guest or not."

A feeling of unease raced through Lin's body. "What about the other woman?"

"She was the owner of the hotel who purchased the place the first time it was auctioned off. The woman was from Boston. Her name was Mara Winslow."

Tiny electric pulses zapped at Lin's skin. "Mara Winslow. Did she spend a lot of time at the hotel?"

"I haven't any information on that," Anton said. "After the fire, a hotel employee told reporters that he wasn't even aware that Mrs. Winslow was at the hotel that night."

"That seems odd," Viv said. "If the hotel owner was on the premises, wouldn't the employees be alerted that she was there?"

Anton shrugged. "Perhaps that wasn't something they did back in the late 1800s."

"Or maybe she spent a lot of time there so it wasn't anything new to the employees," Leonard suggested.

"Do you know anything about Mara Winslow?" Lin asked.

"I didn't have much time to research the woman, but I will do more soon. I found out that Mrs. Winslow was a wealthy woman who made her fortune prior to marriage by owning several shops and apartment buildings in the city. When she married, she and her husband combined their holdings and expanded the business. Her husband died when he was in his early forties and Mara never remarried. I discovered that she had ancestors on Nantucket. I'll look more into that tomorrow."

"So she had a connection to the island," Lin said. "I wonder if she knew the two other people who died in the fire."

The sun had set and Jeff lit the lanterns set around the deck and switched on one of the outside lights creating a warm golden glow around the outdoor table.

"There's a lot to think about," Viv said.

"And a whole lot more to find out," Leonard added.

Lin shivered when a cool breeze wrapped around her and she slipped into her light jacket. "Does anyone need a sweater?"

Everyone thanked Lin, but agreed that they were comfortable sitting out on the deck.

Lin was getting colder by the minute, and realizing the reason why, she turned her head to the field behind the house.

Her ghost-woman stood shimmering in the field staring at Lin. Wearing a long dress with her hair twisted up in a bun ... she wore a sad expression on her face.

Red light poured off the spirit and lit up a circle in the grass around her.

Lin made eye contact with the woman.

*We're trying to help you. We just need more time.*

# 8

Before heading off for her first landscaping job of the morning, Lin and Nicky stopped at Viv's bookstore so she could pick up a coffee. When they entered the busy café, they saw Libby sitting at one of the small tables. The dog went off to look for Queenie while Lin walked over, with coffee in hand, to sit with her distant cousin.

Libby looked up from her phone and took off her reading glasses. "Carolin. Nice to see you. Sit." The woman put her phone aside and gestured to the seat opposite. "I asked Vivian for an update, but she's too busy to talk right now."

Lin gave Libby the summarized version of what had been happening.

"Things are progressing. Good. It's unusual to

see a building from the past the way you did. Your skills are certainly evolving. I'm impressed."

"I was pretty surprised to see the hotel," Lin admitted. "Seeing it really sucked the energy out of me. I was exhausted afterward, and my head felt weird for the rest of the night."

"That's understandable." Libby nodded. "I've reached out to some of my contacts. An acquaintance of mine has some experience with shared dreaming. I believe she'll be coming to the island shortly to speak with us. We can meet with her and discuss the situation."

Lin said, "I think that will be really helpful. It might take some cajoling to get Viv to the meeting, but we'll convince her eventually."

"What about Leonard? Will he be open to a meeting?"

"He'll be fine with it."

"Excellent." Libby took a sip from her mug. "So perhaps, the ghost's name is Mara Winslow. Something about the name sounds familiar to me, but I don't know why. Is Anton going to look into the woman's history?"

"He'll do more research today. I looked her up myself late last night. She had a daughter, Maureen. Mara was forty-five when she died in the fire. Her daughter was twenty and lived in Boston. That's all I could find with a quick search. We'll learn more over the coming days."

"And you mentioned two other people died in the hotel fire. Do you know their names?"

"Anton told us the woman's name was Paulette Simons, age thirty-four, and the man was Lewis Whitman, age fifty. They weren't together. I don't know anything more about them."

"Anton will be helpful in finding out more information. One thing will lead to another until we understand what's going on, what the ghost needs, and why she has appeared to you now. Something is happening that has triggered the visitations." Libby checked the time. "I must be going. I'll let you know when my acquaintance will arrive to meet with us. Have a nice day, Carolin. Call me if you need me ... I don't care what time it is, day or night." Libby kindly patted Lin's shoulder as she hurried away.

Back in her truck with Nicky, Lin decided to make a detour before meeting Leonard at the first client's home. She pulled into the Surfside parking lot and got out.

"I don't know why I'm here, Nick," she told her dog companion. "I just had the urge to stop and look around."

Lin and Nicky walked over to where the bike racks were and as he sniffed at the dune grasses, she stood and looked out over the water. So many things had changed over the years since the hotel was here. A train had run from town to several areas of the island. There was once a restaurant and a train depot right here. Automobiles weren't allowed on Nantucket roads. Then the train had to stop coming to Surfside, and that decision spelled doom for the hotel and the restaurant. The land around Surfside plummeted in value and the people who purchased parcels in the area lost their money. What good was the land when there was no way to get to it?

Lin looked over to where she'd seen the hotel yesterday. She blinked fast several times trying to clear her vision. She stared at the place where it had stood, watching closely to see if she noticed any shimmering particles in the air that might indicate the hotel would materialize.

*Why couldn't the three people who died in the hotel fire escape? Were they all in the same section of the hotel? Did they know each other? Mara must have known the hotel like the back of her hand, and yet, she was unable to get out. What happened? Are our dreams tied to that night? Are the nightmares trying to show us something from the fire? Or does it have nothing to do with what we're trying to help with?*

With a sigh, Lin kept her eyes on the space where the hotel once stood, imagining sitting in a rocking chair on its wide, wraparound porch enjoying the view and the warm, gentle breezes off the ocean. She thought of the woman who had purchased the hotel.

*Are you my ghost? If you are, what do you need from us, Mara? How can we help you?*

Lin's phone buzzed with a text.

*"You sleeping late, Coffin? Do I have to do all the work on my own?*

A smile creeped over Lin's lips. *I'll be right there. On my way.*

Lin and Viv sat on Lin's deck eating dinner together while the cat and dog went out to explore the meadow behind the house. Jeff had gone to Martha's Vineyard overnight to look at a renovation job, and John, a successful island real estate agent, was showing some houses to prospective clients.

"The summer festival will be here before we

know it," Viv said. "I have to get the shop ready for the sidewalk sale."

"You know I'll help you. We'll get it all done in time. We always do."

"And I appreciate it."

"I love the summer festival," Lin said. "All the tourists and the townspeople out and about, the concerts, the sidewalk sale, the farmer's market. It's such a great prelude to summer. I hope it's a nice day."

"Is Jeff still threatening to run the festival's 10k road race?" Viv asked as she sipped from her glass of wine.

"He's determined to do it. He wants me to do it with him."

"You said no, didn't you?" Viv passed the basket of garlic bread to her cousin.

"I said *maybe*."

"*No* is a much better answer. Have you even done any training?"

"No, I haven't, but it's only two more miles than my usual run." Lin sprinkled grated cheese over her spaghetti.

"Two more *long* miles," Viv told her. "Why don't you just cheer Jeff from the sidelines? We can wear spring dresses and stand in the shade at the side of the road with an iced tea in our hands and shout to him about how great he's doing. Doesn't that sound better than running the race?"

Lin chuckled. "You make a convincing argument."

"Darned right I do. I've had years of practice avoiding things like that."

"I was thinking ... after dinner, want to take a ride?" Lin asked.

Viv raised her eyes and stared at her cousin. "Why do I get the feeling I should say no immediately?"

"It's just a car ride, and a stop."

"Oh, no. You want to go to Surfside, don't you? Why? What do you want to do there? I'm sure you're not interested in looking out over the dunes at the ocean to admire the view."

"I just want to look around," Lin said innocently.

Viv took a bite of her salad. "No."

"Why not?"

"Can't we just have a nice meal, and then relax on the sofas and watch a movie together? Can't we have one nice evening without ghosts and buildings that materialize and vanish?" Viv shook her head. "Our lives are so weird."

"We can watch the movie when we get back. I don't want to spend hours there."

"Why don't we go there tomorrow in the daylight. Why does it have to be at night?"

"It's just something to do."

"No."

"Come on. It might be helpful to our investigation," Lin almost whined when she said the sentence. "If we can quickly find out what the ghost wants, then the case will be solved and we can be done with it."

Viv sighed. "I know I've said this a hundred times, and I'll say it a hundred more. Why can't these spirits tell you what they want? Just come out with it. Why does it always have to be so cloak and dagger and mysterious. Just tell us what you want. Everything would be so much easier that way. For all involved."

"If they could communicate with us, they would," Lin said with a shrug.

"Would they? Maybe they enjoy watching you put the puzzle together. Maybe it's a game with them."

"It's not," Lin said.

Viv blew out a breath. "I know it isn't. Okay, okay. I'll go to Surfside with you. But we're only staying for twenty minutes, then it's back here to watch a movie."

Lin smiled. "Okay."

"With popcorn ... *buttered* popcorn."

"Deal."

Viv stood to start clearing away the plates. "I don't know why I let you talk me into these things."

"Because you love me," Lin teased.

In fifteen minutes, the cousins, the dog, and the cat arrived in the truck at Surfside's dark parking lot and walked over to the dunes. The ocean waves pounded the shore with loud booms and the stars sparkled in the night sky. The nearly full moon shined its silvery light along the beach and made a glittering path of diamonds over the water.

"It's a pretty night," Viv observed. "Where did the hotel stand?"

Lin pointed. "There. At the top of those dunes."

"Can you see it? Is it there?" Viv rubbed her arms with her hands.

"No. There isn't anything."

They stayed by the dunes for another fifteen minutes watching the waves and chatting.

"The ghost hasn't shown up either?" Viv asked.

"No." Lin's voice was heavy with disappointment. "I guess we can head back home."

"We can try another time," Viv said encouragingly.

As they turned to walk to the truck, Lin was engulfed by freezing air and she swiveled on her feet to look behind her.

In the spot where the hotel used to be, Emily Witchard Coffin and Sebastian Coffin stood side by side, their eyes pinned onto their descendant. The two ghosts appeared to Lin on occasion and had been helpful in some mysteries she had to solve.

"What is it?" Viv turned to see her cousin looking toward the dunes. "Is someone here?" She moved closer to Lin and held onto her arm.

Nicky wagged his tail as he looked over at the two ghosts.

"It's Emily and Sebastian," Lin whispered without taking her eyes off of them. Her fingers reached for her horseshoe necklace, and despite her skin feeling like ice, her inner core filled with warmth and she heard words form in her mind ... a message from her ancestors.

*When the time comes, do not be afraid.*

# 9

"What the heck does that mean?" Viv asked with a frantic tone. "*When the time comes*? What time? When we're about to die? Don't be afraid when we're facing death?"

"That's all I heard. Well, I don't even really *hear* it when I get a message from Sebastian and Emily. It's more like a mental message that just shows up in my brain." Lin clutched the truck's steering wheel while they sat in the Surfside parking lot.

"What's going to happen?" Viv questioned even though she knew her cousin was unable to provide an answer. "Oh, man."

Lin swallowed hard. "I don't think anyone is going to die. I think the message means that when we face danger we don't need to be afraid."

"Ugh. I hope so." Viv pushed at the side of her light brown hair and attempted to convince herself. "That must be it. We don't need to be afraid when we do whatever it is we have to do. That's what they mean. We'll be okay."

"That's what I think, too." Lin nodded. "Come on. Let's head home."

They were quiet on the drive back to Lin's cottage, and were still silent when they went into the house with the dog and cat, each young woman thinking things over.

"Want some tea?" Lin asked.

Viv agreed and took a seat on one of the stools at the kitchen island. "I feel a little better. I'm not filled with panic. I think the ghosts' message was meant to encourage us, to be supportive. Don't you think so? If there was some chance we'd get killed, they'd warn us about that, wouldn't they? Unless, because they're ghosts they know something awful about our futures and don't want to tell us."

"I think it was meant as a message of encouragement." Lin poured the hot water into the mugs. "Maybe something will be scary, but we don't have to be afraid. Everything will work out." She set a mug in front of her cousin and took a seat next to her.

"I think we're okay," Viv said. "I think we're going

to be fine. The message took me by surprise, that's all, and my mind got carried away and I panicked."

"Me, too." Lin took a swallow of her tea and ran her index finger over her necklace. "Let's stop worrying and do something productive. Let's do an internet search on Paulette Simons and Lewis Whitman."

Lin opened her laptop and keyed the woman's name and the date of 1898 into the search bar. "All that comes up is a historical document listing her name as a victim of the hotel fire. It mentions Lewis Whitman, as well. There isn't anything about their occupations or where they were from. Maybe we need to go to the historical museum and search their files and archives. The library has old news articles and there might be something about the fire."

"We can meet there tomorrow after work," Viv suggested. "Now, how about that movie and popcorn you promised me?"

Soon, the cousins, with a big bowl of buttered popcorn in between them, shared the sofa with the dog and cat while a movie played on the television.

When Lin and Viv walked into the historical museum's library, they spotted Anton Wilson bent over a desktop computer, squinting at the screen. He jumped when the cousins walked up behind him and said his name.

Anton let out a long breath. "I didn't hear you come up. Don't scare me like that."

Lin and Viv took seats on either side of the historian.

"Are you researching the hotel?" Lin asked hopefully.

"I am, yes. I'm looking at hiring contracts for railroad workers and I've been searching for information about the hotel as it fell into decline after the trains stopped running to Surfside. I've also been looking into the backgrounds of the three people who lost their lives in the fire." Anton pointed to the screen. "I've done a little investigating into Mara Winslow's family tree."

Lin looked at the historian with interest. "What did you discover?"

"I found out Mara's great-great-granddaughter has a home here on the island." He passed a small piece of paper to Lin. "Here's the woman's name and contact information. It might be helpful to speak with her."

Lin read the words printed on the paper. *Louella Lowell Martin*. She handed the paper to Viv before asking Anton, "Do you know anything about Ms. Martin?"

Anton glanced at his notes. "She's forty-four years old, has a fifteen-year-old daughter, Angela. Ms. Martin's husband is recently deceased, a car accident. That's all I found before I moved on to the other two people who died in the fire."

"I'll get in touch with her. She might know some family information about Mara."

"The younger woman who perished in the blaze, Paulette Simons, lived in Boston and worked as a nurse," Anton reported. "I don't know why she was on the island. She was a registered guest at the hotel. I haven't found anything to suggest she was with a companion, but if she and a friend had made separate reservations, there wouldn't be a written link between Ms. Simons and someone else in the registration book, so she may have traveled here with a friend or family member, but I just don't know."

"Well, that's more than what Lin and I found about the woman," Viv said. "Maybe she was here for a vacation and some time to herself. Was she married?"

"I don't know. Maybe not. I haven't found an obituary yet for Ms. Simons. But I will."

"What about the man who died?" Lin questioned. "Have you located any information on him?"

Anton swiveled his seat around. "Lewis Whitman. He was a business man. He also lived in Boston. He was involved in real estate development, among other things. I'm going to speculate that he was meeting Mara at the hotel to discuss business of some sort. Maybe the man was interested in buying the hotel."

"Why would he?" Viv asked. "The trains weren't running as frequently as they had been and it must have been evident that they'd stop altogether. With no way to get to the hotel, it would be certain to go out of business. Why would Mr. Whitman invest in a lost cause?"

"Who knows what he was thinking?" Anton shrugged. "Maybe the man was forward thinking and had some plans for the hotel and the land that didn't require train transportation."

"I wonder what that could have been," Lin thought aloud as a little wave of unease ran through her. "Anyway, you think Mr. Whitman went to the hotel to speak to Ms. Winslow about buying it?"

"It crossed my mind as a possibility," Anton said.

"But his visit might not have had anything to do with business at all. He could have been visiting the island in order to relax and take some time off."

"Was he visiting here with a companion?" Lin asked. "Did you find anything that linked him to someone else staying at the hotel?"

"His name was the only one on the register assigned to the room he was staying in."

"Were the three victims staying in the same section of the hotel?" Viv asked.

"I haven't found a layout of the place yet." Anton shook his head. "I will find a schematic of it eventually. However, the room numbers suggest to me that Ms. Simons and Mr. Whitman were indeed in the same part of the hotel. My guess is that Ms. Winslow probably had an owner's suite, but where it was located within the building, I don't know."

"We had a visit last night from two familiar people." Viv eyed Anton.

The man's eyebrows raised above the frames of his eyeglasses. "Emily and Sebastian? You saw them, Vivian?"

"I didn't see them. Only Lin did. They had a message for her."

Anton turned to stare at Lin. "What message did you receive? Was it another *mental* message?"

"It was." Lin gave a nod. "It was only one sentence that formed in my mind."

"Well, tell me what it was. What did they say to you?"

"When the time comes, don't be afraid."

"How would you interpret that?" Viv asked the historian, her voice shaking a little with worry.

Anton blinked at her. "I think it's fairly straightforward, isn't it? Don't be afraid."

"But does it mean, don't be afraid as you die?"

"What?" Anton sat up straight. "They didn't mention anything in the message about dying. My take is that you will have something you must do or help with and it might be a scary situation, but have no fear, you will be all right."

"Is that really what you think?" Viv pressed.

"Yes, it is."

"You don't think something terrible is going to happen to me, Lin, and Leonard?"

"That idea did not enter my mind."

"You're not just saying that, are you?"

"Really, Vivian, the idea of your demise had no place in my interpretation."

"Okay, good. Just checking." Viv's shoulders seemed to relax.

"Of course, what do I know?" Anton kidded, and

chuckled when he saw the look of horror on Viv's face.

Viv and Lin left the museum library without Anton who had planned to stay until closing time. Streetlamps were just flickering on and the sun was hanging at the horizon when the cousins descended the steps to the sidewalk.

Halfway down the granite stairs, Lin stopped.

When Viv noticed Lin wasn't walking beside her, she turned back. "What? Did you forget something inside?"

Lin shook her head slowly as her eyes seemed to fix on a point across the street.

"Lin?"

When Lin gestured with her chin to the other side of the road, Viv understood and she scurried up the steps to stand next to her cousin. "It's not Emily and Sebastian again with some new, frightening message for us, is it?"

"It's my ghost," Lin whispered. "She must be Mara Winslow."

Glowing red, the ghost held Lin's eyes for several minutes before fading away.

"She's gone."

Lin and Viv descended the steps.

"Did Mara tell you anything? Did she give you a

message?"

"No, she didn't. She just stared at me. But I need to call Mara's descendant, Louella Martin, and set up a meeting for us to speak with her."

Viv eyed her cousin thinking Mara certainly did give Lin a message.

# 10

Louella Lowell Martin's home was located mid-island on a quiet, shady street of nicely cared-for ranches and Cape-style houses on modest lots. Louella's house resembled Lin's cottage, but also had a pretty front porch with window boxes on the railings and flower pots lining the steps. There was a *for sale* sign stuck in the lawn beside the sidewalk.

Louella came out the front door with a white cat following behind her. The woman was forty-four years old, petite, with auburn hair cut to chin-length and hazel eyes. She waved to the cousins who were getting out of Lin's truck, and introductions were made when they met on the porch.

"What a lovely house," Lin told her.

"I love flowers so sometimes I go a little overboard with pots and gardens. I think flowers make a place seem welcoming and homey. I haven't had much time to work on my gardens this spring." Louella had full cheeks and a round face that gave the impression she was a kind, friendly person.

"Well, everything looks beautiful," Viv said as she admired the boxes and planters overflowing with blooms.

"Would you like to come inside? We could sit on the back porch," Louella suggested. She led the way through a nicely-decorated interior into a small, but updated kitchen with high-end cabinetry, wood floors, polished countertops and huge windows letting in the light. There were sliding doors leading to a covered porch that extended the width of the house. The back lawn was green and lush and a border of plants and flowers edged the property line.

"This is gorgeous." Viv's eyes swept around the space admiring the landscaping.

"Do you do all of this yourself?" Lin marveled at the woman's expertise.

Louella's face clouded. "I usually do, but this year, I haven't had the time. I might need to hire someone to take over for me."

"Lin owns a landscaping company," Viv shared.

"She and her partner are the best around. She and her partner do the most amazing work."

Lin looked a little embarrassed by her cousin's praise. She told Louella, "I think we should be hiring you, not the other way around."

"Have a seat. I'll get some refreshments." The woman darted into the house and returned a few minutes later carrying a tray with a pitcher of iced tea, a carafe of lemonade, and a plate of cookies which she set on the wicker table.

After she poured the drinks, Louella said, "I was very surprised to get your call. I never expected anyone would have an interest in my great-great-grandmother."

"We recently learned about the Surf Hotel," Lin explained. "I'd heard a few mentions of it when I was growing up, but never really paid attention to it. Surfside is my favorite beach on the island. My husband and I are doing some renovations to our house and we found an old booklet my grandfather had saved. The booklet was done by the historical society and had old photos of some of Nantucket's homes and buildings along with a short description about them. When I saw the picture of the hotel, it piqued my interest, and a friend of ours who is a historian told us you were a relative of one of the hotel's owners."

"Yes. Mara Winslow. She owned the hotel for a short time. It had lost its luster and she wanted to return it to its former elegant state, but the timing was bad. The train schedule had been cut and it wasn't long until the trains no longer serviced that part of the island which meant the end for any businesses located in the Surfside area that depended on the tourist trade."

"We understand there was a fire," Viv said.

Louella nodded. "Mara had owned the hotel for about two years. She'd put a good deal of money into it and it was again a beautiful place to stay. Unfortunately, that's when the trains cut back, and shortly after that, the fire destroyed about half the hotel. There was no reason to try and rebuild since there was so little train service. A section of the hotel collapsed, and in 1900 or 1901, someone else bought the place. It's a sad tale. The hotel my ancestor loved ended up claiming her life." Louella slowly shook her head and glanced out to the garden. "Imagine what that place would be worth now, if it had been in operation all these years."

"Mara was from Boston?" Lin asked.

"She was. She owned land, shops, and buildings

that she rented out. Mara had inherited money and holdings when her parents passed away and she expanded and built the business. She must have been a smart woman and a very good businessperson. Mara became very wealthy. She married in her mid-twenties and had one daughter, Maureen."

"Did your family spend time here? Was it a family tradition to visit Nantucket?" Lin questioned.

"I don't think my grandparents came here very much. My mother didn't either until my husband and I bought this house. My husband and I came to the island before we were married. We were both interested in seeing it since my relative had owned the hotel here. We fell in love with the place and about ten years later, we were able to buy this house. My mother comes often. She loves the island."

"We noticed a for sale sign out front," Lin said. "Are you moving to another house here?"

Louella's face looked like it was about to crumple, but she straightened her shoulders and took a deep breath. "Like my ancestor, Mara, my family has suffered a tragedy." The woman swallowed before going on. "A few months ago, my husband and daughter were driving along the highway outside of Boston when a tractor-trailer truck jack-knifed on the road and flipped over causing a multi-car accident. My husband was killed. Our daughter was badly injured." Louella wiped at her moist eyes.

Lin and Viv were stunned by this news and murmured their condolences.

Louella wrung her hands together. "My husband was a lawyer. He had his own practice. It was just him, he didn't have any lawyers working for him, just a secretary and a part-time paralegal. As it turned out, we were heavily in debt. I had no idea. I work part-time in a doctor's office doing billing. There is no way I can afford the debt we have. My daughter's surgeries and health care is and will continue to be extremely expensive. I've put this house and our house located in a Boston suburb on the market. It breaks my heart to lose our homes, but there are far more pressing issues to deal with right now."

"I'm very, very sorry to hear what you're going through," Lin said softly.

"We hope your daughter will get better soon," Viv told the woman. "How old is she?"

"Angela is fifteen. She broke both legs, suffered a head injury, had internal damage and bleeding. She's looking at years of recovery." Louella tried unsuccessfully to smile. "But we'll get through it. We have to."

Lin's heart was full of sorrow for the woman and

her losses. "I'm so sorry to bother you when you're going through so much. We had no idea. We wouldn't have gotten in touch, if we'd known you have so much going on."

"No, no. I'm glad you did. Talking with both of you is a nice break from everything. I'm happy you're here. What else can I answer for you?"

Lin was unsure if they should continue their conversation or if it would be better for her and Viv to leave, but Louella seemed sincere when she told them she was enjoying their visit, so she went ahead and asked another question.

"Have you heard the names Paulette Simons or Lewis Whitman?"

Louella's face scrunched up in thought and was about to answer in the negative, when recognition showed in her eyes.

"Oh, they were the ones who died in the hotel fire with Mara."

"That's what we've read," Viv nodded. "Do you know anything about them?"

"I really don't. I think Mr. Whitman was a businessman who might have known Mara from Boston."

"Any idea why he was at the hotel? Was it a business visit? A short vacation for him?" Lin asked.

"I really don't know."

"What about Paulette Simons? Do you know anything about her? Did she know Mara?"

Again, Louella shook her head. "I don't know." Her face brightened. "But you know what? My mother is coming in a couple of days to help me pack up some things and get some other things taken care of. She might know some answers to those questions. She loves history and loves learning things about our family tree. She might have some information to share with you. Would you like to come back when she's here?"

"We don't want to intrude," Lin said.

A little smile crossed Louella's face. "My mother would love to talk to you. You might end up being sorry you asked her anything because she will definitely talk your ears off."

Lin and Viv chuckled.

"If it wouldn't be any trouble and your mother is up for a visit, we'd love to speak with her." Lin gave Louella her contact information.

"She'll be arriving the day after tomorrow. We have some things to get done, but I'll call you in a few days and we can set a time to meet."

After some conversation, Lin and Viv thanked

Louella for her time, again offered their sympathies for what she was dealing with, and left the house.

They sat in the truck for a few minutes before heading back to town.

"I feel so badly for her," Viv said. "What a mess she's in. Everything was going along fine, and then disaster struck them. What a terrible thing to lose her husband and have her daughter so badly injured. I felt like crying when she was telling us about it."

"Me, too," Lin agreed. "A split second can change everything."

As she reached for the ignition to start the truck and pull away from the curb, Lin saw something out of the corner of her eye.

Glowing red, Mara Winslow's ghost stood on the front lawn of Louella's house watching Lin and Viv drive away.

# 11

It was an unseasonably warm day so Lin, Jeff, Viv, and John decided to head to the beach for the afternoon to swim, play bocce on the sand, and sun themselves. There were quite a few other people who had the same idea and the beach looked vibrant with blankets, chairs, and towels spread out under brightly colored umbrellas. After the long cold winter, it was uplifting to return to the beach to have fun and relax.

As they carried their things down the slope to the sand, Lin glanced at the spot near the dunes where the hotel once stood, but nothing was visible.

"You don't see anything do you?" Viv asked.

"Nothing. Maybe today will be quiet and uneventful."

Viv shook her head. "Hopefully, but I wouldn't count on it."

The waves were big, and once they dropped their chairs and towels, Jeff and John raced each other into the water.

"They're like little kids." Viv laughed.

"Shall we join them?" Lin eyed the white foam glistening as the waves crested and broke against the shore.

"Really? It's going to be cold."

"We can't let the guys have all the fun."

The cousins shared impish looks and then tore down the beach, screaming with delight as they leapt over the waves and dove into the ocean.

When they came up for air, Viv said, "It's not as bad as I thought it would be."

Lin agreed. "Yeah. It's only my feet that feel like blocks of ice."

Jeff and John swam over to join them and they spent forty minutes riding the waves and floating on their backs looking up at the clear, blue sky.

Back on the beach, they toweled off and sat in the sand chairs enjoying the picnic lunch of grilled chicken sandwiches, cut-up veggies and hummus, slices of watermelon, and ginger-molasses cookies they'd brought along.

Munching on a cookie, John said, "Viv had a crazy dream last night."

Lin looked at her cousin with concern. "What was it about?"

Viv dipped her carrot in the hummus. "I don't remember much about it."

John gave Lin a worried look. "*You* were in the dream."

Viv gave her husband a poke in the arm. "I wasn't going to share the dream with her."

Jeff and Lin exchanged nervous glances.

"Why weren't you going to share it?" Jeff asked.

With a heavy sigh, Viv shook her head. "I don't think every detail of these stupid dreams needs to be discussed. Some things are meaningless. There isn't any point in going over each and every dream we have."

"It could be important to go over every detail." Lin approached the topic with caution. "Did you have one of our dark, upsetting dreams?"

"I keep having them every night." Viv's voice was soft.

"Was this one different than the usual ones?"

"A little."

"Just tell her," John suggested. "This whole shared dream thing freaks me out. I can't wrap my head around it, but it's better not to hide from these nightmares. Just put it out there. It might be important."

Viv blew the air out of her lungs. "Okay, okay." She raised her eyes to Lin. "The dream was the same as always. I'm in the dark. I can't see anything. I'm trying to run, but I keep stumbling and I can't make my feet move. I need to find someone who needs me." She stopped talking and paused for a few moments. "I think you were in the dream. I saw a door. I saw fire and smoke. I think you were trapped on the other side of the door."

Lin's heart dropped and a chill ran over her skin. "Could you see me?"

"No. But I heard you calling to me." Viv almost looked ashamed of her dream. "Maybe it's because we've been talking so much about the old hotel and the fire that a fire made its way into my nightmare."

Lin didn't say anything.

Jeff asked Viv, "Did you reach Lin? Did you get the door opened in the dream?"

"I don't know. I woke up before I found out."

John added, "She woke up screaming."

Lin swallowed hard and cleared her throat, and she tried to keep worry and emotion out of her voice.

"It could be an important clue. Could you tell where we were? Do you know the building we were in?"

Again, Viv shook her head. "I don't know. It was too dark and smoky to see where I was."

"Was Leonard there?" Jeff asked.

"I didn't see or hear him."

Lin reached out and touched her cousin's arm. "We need to share what happens in the nightmares. It's okay. If we talk about the little changes we experience, we can focus on what's going on and what the dreams are trying to convey to us. We can't toss out clues because they make us uncomfortable. We need all the information we can get."

"I know," Viv said. "I only wish the details didn't involve any of us in dangerous situations."

Lin forced a smile. "We'll be okay. All of us." After taking a drink from her water container, she said, "I think we should get together with Leonard soon to go over what's changed in our dreams. He doesn't like talking about it when we're working. I think he'll be more open to discussing the nightmares if we make a specific time to meet to go over new details together."

"Okay. That sounds good. Maybe we should invite Libby and Anton to the meeting," Viv said.

"They might be able to help us interpret what we're dreaming about."

"I'll ask them to join us." Lin took her phone from her beach bag, and she and Viv chose a few dates and times, and then Lin sent texts to the others asking when they might be able to meet.

John took a slice of watermelon from the container. "I didn't hear how your meeting went with Louella Lowell Martin."

Lin and Viv took turns summarizing what they'd learned.

"Her house has been put on the market," Lin said.

John pouted. "Why didn't she call me to work as her real estate agent?"

"She doesn't know you," Viv tried to be reasonable. "Maybe she knows the agent she listed the house with."

When John asked who the listing went to, he made a face. "Louella will be sorry she didn't go with my agency. Why is she selling the place?"

When Viv explained the reason, John's face fell. "That's terrible. That poor family."

"It's pretty clear Louella has some serious financial problems," Lin said. "They're also selling the house they own outside of Boston. Her husband had a great deal of debt and the daughter's medical expenses will be very high. Louella seems to be in a real jam."

"And she only works part-time doing medical billing," Viv added. "She can't really increase her work hours or look for another job because her daughter requires so much care."

"Selling the houses should be a help," Jeff offered.

"I think it will help eliminate the debt her husband accumulated," Lin said. "But paying that off might eat up all the profits from the sales. Louella is going to be in a bind due to the medical costs the daughter will incur."

"Bad luck," John sighed. "Things can go wrong in the blink of an eye."

"I saw Mara's ghost when we left the historical museum and again when we left Louella's house," Lin said. "Both times, Mara just stared at me. I like to think that when she shows up, it means we're on the right track looking for information."

"Or," Viv kidded, "it means you are completely off the rails."

Everyone chuckled.

"If that's the case, then Mara needs to give me a little bit more help," Lin said. She looked out at the sparkling ocean where people were swimming or playing at the edge of the water and thought how lucky they all were. So often, we don't count our blessings. We forget to be grateful for the people who are so important to us, for all that we have.

Jeff asked Lin to go for a walk along the beach with him, and John and Viv decided to stay on the blanket and take quick naps.

The couple walked hand in hand along the sand, enjoying the almost-hot sunny day off from work. Jeff told Lin more details about the renovation jobs he and Kurt would be bidding on. "I'm excited about working on those homes. They're both beautiful antiques. I really hope we get the jobs." He described the homes and what would be done to bring them back to their glory.

Lin smiled at her husband. "You don't ever tire of renovating? You work all day doing it and then you have to come home and do it there, too."

"I love the work," Jeff said. "Taking something and making it beautiful and functional, it's almost like creating a work of art. And people get to enjoy the new spaces. I think I have the best job in the world."

"That's one of the things I love about you. You're always so positive and excited about whatever you're working on, from a doggy door to a full renovation on a mansion. You always put your very best into each creation."

"You and Leonard do the same thing with your landscaping. You two always make the world a little bit more beautiful. I guess we all have a lot in common."

When they returned to their spot on the beach, Viv and John were just waking up, and everyone collected their things to head home. Walking up the sandy slope to the Surfside parking lot, Lin caught a whiff of smoke ... right before she heard a woman scream.

Whipping around toward the direction of the shout, she saw the ghost-hotel, its atoms shimmering and glowing red.

Flames shot from the roof and smoke billowed into the sky.

And then it was gone ... leaving Lin shaking and distressed.

# 12

Early the next morning, Lin and Viv sat around the deck table at Anton's house while Nicky trotted about the yard sniffing here and there before resting in the shade of a big oak tree.

"I came across some old letters written by Mara Winslow and Paulette Simons." The historian had his laptop propped on the table and was navigating to the document he wanted. "It was purely by luck that I found them."

"So they knew each other," Viv said watching the man type on his keyboard.

"Did you get a sense of their relationship from their letters?" Lin asked waiting not very patiently for Anton to tell them some details of what he'd found. “Was it a professional relationship? A friendship?”

Anton ignored the questions and focused on his screen. “Both women lived in Boston. As we know, Paulette was a nurse. From what I’ve gleaned from the letters, Mara fell on some ice one winter and broke her ankle and some bones in her foot. Paulette was hired as a private duty nurse to help her so that’s how they knew one another. It seems a friendship developed between the women. After Mara healed and was able to manage on her own again, Paulette left for other jobs.”

“But Paulette stayed in Boston?” Lin asked.

“She did, yes.”

“When did Mara fall? How long had they known each other before the fire took their lives?”

“About ten years.” Anton stared at the laptop screen. “Mara did a great deal of traveling and wrote often to Paulette about the places she was visiting, what she was doing, what she was seeing. It seems Mara and Paulette shared a love of art. Whenever Mara visited a museum, she shared what she’d seen in remarkable detail. There aren’t that many letters that have survived, but there are enough to get a sense of their friendship.”

“Where did you find the letters?” Lin questioned,

a little surprised that any correspondence of theirs had remained from over a hundred years ago.

“Some were in an American historical archive and others I found reprinted in a book written by a historian I know. I’ve contacted my associate to see if there were other letters she didn’t include in her book. She’s going to look through her notes for me.”

“When the fire broke out, Paulette must have been at the hotel as a guest of Mara’s,” Viv guessed. “Is there anything in the letters that suggest the two women visited Nantucket together at other times?”

“I found one mention in a letter from Mara to Paulette. Mara was probably spending a good deal of time on-island when she first purchased the hotel to plan and oversee the renovations,” Anton told them. “In the letter to Paulette, she talks about the beauty of Surfside and how magnificent the hotel will be once the updates are made to it. Paulette must have visited Mara here to see the hotel and to hear about the plans for its renewal. Paulette must have been here for another visit when the fire destroyed half the hotel.”

Something prickly ran through Lin’s muscles. “I don’t know.”

Viv and Anton turned to the young woman.

"What don't you know?" Viv's eyes had clouded with worry.

"I think Paulette was at the hotel for another reason."

"Like what?" Viv kept her eyes on her cousin's face. "Do you have some idea about why she was here on-island?"

"Not really. But I have a feeling it wasn't simply a pleasant visit to see her friend. I think the reason she was here could be important."

Anton's forehead was crinkled in thought.

Lin asked the historian, "Have you found any link between Mara and Lewis Whitman?"

Blinking as he turned his thoughts from the reasons Paulette may have been at the hotel to Lin's question, Anton shook his head. "Not yet. He was a business person, and Mara was a business person. They both lived in Boston. They may have known each other through the business community. I'll be looking for anything that may link the two."

Viv's eyes widened. "Could they have been in a relationship?"

"Interesting," Anton commented.

Lin considered the idea. "That could have been the case. Mara's husband passed away years before Mara died in the fire. She and Lewis Whitman could have been seeing each other. Maybe they had plans to marry. Maybe he came out to help with ideas for the hotel."

"What could they do to save the hotel?" Viv asked. "Transportation from town to Surfside was almost non-existent, or was about to be soon."

Lin sat straighter. "Could they have moved the hotel from Surfside to a lot close to town? Would that have been possible?"

"Sure, it was possible," Anton said. "The hotel had been disassembled on the mainland and was shipped over here on barges. It could be done again to move it to the center of the island."

"So maybe Mara and Whitman were considering that," Viv said. "It might have been a smart financial thing to do."

"Some things seem like they might be coming together," Lin observed. "Maybe our shared dreams can shed some light on what was happening at the time when Mara must have been considering her options on how to save the hotel. Or maybe other letters will come to light that can give us more information on the three people who died in the fire."

"I'll keep looking. I'll see what else there is to find." Anton nodded. "I'll see you tomorrow evening when we meet to hear and discuss the new details the three of you have experienced in your nightmares."

After leaving Anton's house, Lin and Viv decided to go for a walk and headed through the pretty neighborhoods of town with Nicky happily trotting in front of them. They walked up the slope to the top of Sunset Hill where the oldest house on Nantucket, a National Historic Landmark, was located.

The cousins turned left onto the grounds where a green meadow led them to the dwelling built in 1686 for Jethro Coffin. Still on its original site, the house was constructed as a wedding gift for Jethro and his wife, Mary Gardner, whose marriage brought together two of the oldest island families. The home was built with lumber from the Coffin family on land given to the couple from the Gardners. Eventually the house was abandoned in the late 1800s and it fell into disrepair, but was saved by the island historical society.

Lin loved the old house and the surrounding meadows where wildflowers were blooming, and the huge beautiful tree standing in the front field. A raised bed kitchen garden was located near the old house where plants grew in a recreation of a 1700s vegetable and herb garden. The house itself had a large center chimney with an upside down horseshoe in the middle of it.

The same design could be seen built into the bricks on the chimneys of several old houses on the island and was intended to ward off witches and evil spells. Lin's ancestor, Sebastian Coffin, had the design constructed into the chimney of his own house, but not to keep witches away ... he used the symbol to draw people who had been accused of witchcraft to his home where he and his wife, Emily, provided them with a safe place to stay and helped them build new lives on the island. Lin's necklace showed the same upside down horseshoe on her antique pendant.

No matter how many times they'd been in the house previously, if it wasn't open when they visited, the cousins always peered in the windows to look inside before walking around the grounds.

The day was warm and sunny as Lin and Viv checked out the kitchen garden behind the old house and then sat on the bench under the big tree before heading over to the sandwich shop on the other side of the fields.

"Don't you love living in a place that has so much

of our family history?" Viv glanced around at the house and the flowers in the field.

With a smile, Lin nodded. "It makes me feel grounded, and like I'm never, ever alone. So many of our ancestors walked the same places we do now."

"What do you think about Mara? Do you think she was in a relationship with Lewis Whitman?"

"It's a real possibility," Lin said. "But it could have been purely a business relationship. I wonder if Mara had some sort of plan to keep the hotel going."

"You mean like moving the hotel, like we talked about with Anton?" Viv asked.

"Yeah. Or maybe she had some other ideas. It seems she was a good businesswoman. Do you think it's strange that the three of them were at the hotel during the fire? Were Mara, Paulette, and Lewis there to meet with one another for some reason?"

"What reason would require the three of them at the same meeting?" Viv asked. "Why would Paulette be involved with that? She probably didn't have any money to invest. At least, not the amount of money that would be needed to keep the hotel going."

A terrible thought crossed Lin's mind. "Do you think someone set the hotel on fire? Do you think someone wanted Mara dead?"

"You think she was murdered?" Viv sucked in a

breath of air. "Why would someone want to kill her?"

"I don't know. It might be worth considering."

"Well, if you're considering new ideas, here's another one," Viv said. "What if Mara set the hotel on fire so she could collect the insurance? She knew that a lack of transportation to the hotel would ruin her business so burning it down could have solved her financial problems."

"This is becoming more complicated," Lin sighed. "So the hotel fire was either an accident or...."

Viv finished the sentence. "Or ... it wasn't."

# 13

Even though the sun was setting, the evening was still warm and dry as Lin, Viv, Leonard, and Jeff sat around the fire pit together roasting marshmallows and enjoying cold drinks. Nicky and Queenie alternated between playing in the back field, sitting on the deck, and going inside the house through the doggy door. Anton and Libby had spent the day on the mainland and would be late to the meeting due to a delayed ferry.

The intent of the gathering was to discuss the shared dreams, but Lin and Jeff thought it would relax everyone if they could sit around and chat before turning to the necessary discussion. They talked about the upcoming summer solstice festival, the warm weather, the tourist season, Jeff and Kurt's new business, and some big landscaping projects Lin and Leonard had coming up.

Viv slumped a little in her chair. "Well, shall we get down to it?"

Leonard's face stiffened as he shifted uncomfortably in his patio chair.

"Has anyone's nightmare changed in some ways since they started?" Lin asked after setting her drink down in the lawn next to her.

"Lin knows mine have taken a new turn." Viv pushed at her hair.

Leonard's face looked wary.

Viv explained. "For the past few nights, I've seen a little more than just darkness all around me. It's still dark and I can barely see, but now I'm able to see a door. There's fire and smoke all around." The young woman swallowed hard. "I can hear Lin calling me. She's behind the door. She's trying to get out. I can't move my feet. I can't get to her, no matter how hard I try. I start to sob." Viv passed her hand over her face. "That's when I wake up screaming."

The others kept their eyes pinned on Viv, but no one spoke for nearly a minute.

"You've had this nightmare for a few days?" Leonard asked, his voice hoarse.

Viv nodded, and asked the man, "Have your dreams changed at all?"

Lifting his beer mug to his lips, Leonard took several gulps before placing the glass on one of the rocks encircling the fire pit. "Yeah. Same as yours."

Viv leaned forward with a look of alarm. "You've been dreaming about a fire? Lin's in your dream, too?"

Leonard nodded. "So are you."

"What do you mean?" Lin wanted clarification. "Viv's in the dream?"

With resignation in his voice, Leonard took a deep breath. "You're both in the dream. I can barely see anything. There's smoke and fire. You're both behind the door. You're both shouting for me to help you get out."

Viv's face paled and she sat back in her chair looking stricken. "Oh, gosh." She quickly looked to her cousin. "Have your dreams changed?"

Lin glanced over at her husband, and Jeff gave a nod.

With her hands holding tight to the arm rests of her Adirondack chair, Lin said, "You're both in my dreams. It started two nights ago. Viv and I are trapped in the smoke and fire and we can't get the door open. I don't know where we are. I can only see the door ... it's shrouded in smoke. We're coughing, choking. We yank on the door, but it won't budge. I have something in my hand, but I don't know what it is." She looked at Leonard. "We're desperate. We're yelling for you to save us."

"Is that when you wake up?" Leonard asked. "Or do I get you both out of there?"

"I wake up before you can get us out," Lin told him.

Viv's words sounded shaky when she spoke. "What does this mean? Are we going to be trapped in a fire? Where are we? What's going on? And what does it have to do with this new ghost?"

Leonard ran his hand through his hair. "Did the ghost show up to warn us? Is she trying to help us because she was in a fire, too?"

Lin's mind raced. "If the ghost *is* Mara Winslow, and I think she is, what does she want from us? She died in a fire, but that was over a hundred years ago. What does she want us to do?"

Jeff said, "Her appearance doesn't seem to have any historical significance. It isn't an important anniversary of the hotel, or of train transportation slowing down. It isn't the anniversary of Mara's death either so that can't be why she has suddenly shown up."

Despite feeling shaken by the realization that all three of them were having the same nightmare, Lin asked, "Can you tell what we're wearing in the dream? Are we dressed up for an occasion or are we in casual clothes?

Both Viv and Leonard shook their heads.

Lin asked another question. "Have either of you noticed anything about the space we're in? Is it a house, a barn, a warehouse, a restaurant? Are there any hints at all about where we are?"

Leonard said, "No idea." Viv agreed with him.

"Can you tell the time of day?"

"It's dark where we are, but that might be due to the smoke and fire," Viv said. "I can't tell if it's day or night."

"Well, the dreams have changed," Lin said with a sigh. "We're finding out new information. That will probably continue, so we need to keep our eyes open for any little thing that's different."

"I really hate this." Leonard's jaw tightened. "It's like we're slowly being tortured with awful images that foretell our demise."

Reaching out and touching her friend's arm, Lin said gently, "I think we're seeing this stuff in order to save us."

Leonard's eyes got watery. "Over my dead body … I'm not letting anything happen to you two. I'm not."

Lin's throat tightened with emotion and it prevented her from saying what she wanted to say, so she stood up, stepped over to the man and hugged him, just as a tear escaped from Viv's eye and rolled down her cheek before she lifted her hand and brushed it away.

"And I won't let anything happen to either of you." When Lin held out her hand with her palm facing down, Leonard placed his hand on hers, and Viv reached over and set her hand over theirs. "All for one. We're in this together, and we'll get out of it together."

Nearly blubbering, Viv told them, "Enough with this love-fest. Let's go inside and make some coffee and take a break for a few minutes."

With the tension broken, the others chuckled and agreed, and they filed into the kitchen to see the dog and cat sound asleep curled together on Nicky's dog bed in the corner of the room.

"Sweet and peaceful," Lin said.

Viv's heart warmed at the sight of the animals sleeping so cozily and close together. "No troubles to worry them."

Leonard smiled. “Nothing in the world like friendship and love.”

Looking over at her friend with a tender expression, Lin said, “You’re nothing like I thought you were when we first met.”

“You thought I was a killer, Coffin, so that ain’t saying much.”

Everyone laughed.

Setting up the coffee maker, Jeff told them, “Just goes to show that sometimes first impressions can be deceiving.”

Lin stared at her husband as a flash of unease raced over her skin. *Are our first impressions in this case confusing us?*

After sipping their coffees and munching on some cookies, the mood lightened and they started to feel less stressed so they carried their mugs back outside and, once again, took their seats around the fire pit. The sky was now inky black and some stars sparkled overhead.

When Anton flew around the back corner of the house and hurried over to the group, Nicky and Queenie darted to greet the man. “I’m sorry for being late. Libby has a headache and isn’t going to make it. What have I missed?”

The four people smiled at the man.

Leonard said, "A whole ton of terrible."

Anton stared at them with his jaw slightly agape. "What's happened now?"

"Well, this is all truly fascinating and incredible." Anton looked with wonder from person to person after he'd heard the news about the shared nightmares. "You never cease to amaze me."

Next, Lin and Viv discussed their ideas that the hotel fire was not an accident.

Anton pushed his glasses up his nose and squared his shoulders. "How did those ideas slip past me? Perhaps Mara did indeed set the fire to try and receive the insurance proceeds. She may have been clever in how she set it. The authorities may have missed the details that would have pointed to arson. And if Mara *didn't* set the fire, you are quite correct that someone may have deliberately set the hotel ablaze in order to kill her. So many twists and turns to consider. I must go back to research the cause of the fire. I skipped over that information with my preconceived notions that it was accidental. That was a critical mistake, and one I rarely make."

Lin made an effort to keep a smile from her face.

Anton asked, "Why would someone want Mara dead? Have you considered the reasons someone might attempt to kill the woman? Is that why she's always putting off a red color? Is her rage manifesting as a red aura?"

"We don't know why someone might have wanted to kill her," Viv said. "We really don't know much about her so we can't even guess what a motive might be."

Lin thought about what Anton had said. "I don't think the red aura comes from Mara being angry, but I haven't figured out which mood or emotion the red color is giving off. Maybe it represents the fire that took her life."

"What emotions do you feel from the woman?" Anton questioned.

Pausing to consider what she'd felt from the ghost before giving her reply, Lin said, "I don't feel any rage when Mara appears. I sense concern, worry, a need for help. I don't feel regret or sorrow from her. She needs help, but I can't figure out what she wants us to do for her."

Viv said, "Mara's great-great granddaughter has lost her husband recently and her daughter will require surgeries and rehabilitation from the accident, but there isn't anything we can do to help her with that."

"Mara must need aid of a different kind," Anton suggested.

Lin's heart sank. *But what kind is it?*

# 14

"I'm something of an amateur historian as far as our family goes," Annabelle Lowell, Louella's mother, told Lin and Viv. "I've spent countless hours researching our family's genealogy. It's fascinating to dig into the past and learn about our ancestors." Seventy-four-year old Annabelle was petite and slender and her white-gray hair was cut in a chin-length bob. She seemed energetic, friendly, and pleasant. "When Lou told me she'd spoken with two young women who had an interest in Mara Winslow, I was very surprised. I've been so looking forward to meeting both of you."

Lin explained that she'd found a booklet in her grandfather's things about the Surf Hotel and learned that Mara had purchased the place with the hopes of refurbishing it. She left out the part about seeing Mara's ghost.

"We were intrigued by a businesswoman taking on such a project in the late 1800s and wanted to know more about her," Lin said.

"How can I help?" Annabelle asked. "What have you learned so far?"

Viv said, "We understand Mara purchased the hotel and invested a good amount of money in revitalizing the place, but then train service to the Surfside area was cut back and that caused problems for tourists trying to reach the hotel. We know cars weren't allowed on the island back then."

"From what I've read," Annabelle said, "Mara could see the writing on the wall. She knew the trains would eventually stop servicing the area. She was determined to find a way to keep the hotel going."

"Do you know what ideas she had?" Lin asked.

"She was interested in an alternate means of transportation. She hadn't figured it out yet, at least, in the letters I've found, but she was really thinking about starting something herself to transport visitors from the town to the Surfside area."

"What could she do?" Viv asked. "Cars were

prohibited and erosion threatened the train tracks. What else could be done?"

"She had a notion about using a train-like vehicle that wouldn't require tracks, but would run over the roads. It would pull a wagon. It was going to be more like a trolley-type thing. The letters I've read spoke of the possibility, but it was all at the early planning stages," Annabelle explained.

"Do you think it could have been feasible?" Lin questioned.

Annabelle smiled. "It seems Mara had quite the head for business. She'd planned and invested in many successful ventures before acquiring the hotel, and I certainly wouldn't have bet against her. But unfortunately, fate had different plans."

"We've heard that two other people died in the fire along with your ancestor," Lin said. "Paulette Simons and Lewis Whitman. Do you know anything about them?"

With a nod, Annabelle said, "Paulette was a nurse. She took care of Mara for a couple of months after she broke her ankle. They became friends. I don't know if Paulette traveled with Mara here to the island or if Paulette came to visit her. Unfortunately, they both perished in the blaze. As for Mr. Whitman, I know that he lived in Boston and was also an investor and a businessman. I've always wondered if Whitman was at the hotel to present a business proposition to Mara. From what I've learned about her, I know she was a very independent woman. I'd love to know what she thought about taking on an investor. Would she have taken Whitman on as a partner or would she have sent him packing?"

"What do you think she would have done?" Viv asked.

"I think Mara wanted to be in charge of whatever she was involved with." Annabelle's eyes twinkled. "I don't think she would have taken a partner. I think she was the sink or swim type of person, and if she couldn't do it on her own, she wouldn't have done it at all. Even her husband admired Mara's business sense. Before they married, he wasn't nearly as successful with his ventures as she was with hers."

"Mara owned businesses of her own before marrying?" Viv asked.

"She sure did. She went to college and finished in two years. Her father gave her some money to start her first venture, but after that, everything she did, she did on her own. She used her father's seed money well and the money just rolled in. She married Jacob Bullard Winslow and they had a daughter, but that sure didn't slow her down. She bought and sold property and businesses, she invested, she made deals. Her husband couldn't hold a candle to her. Mara was a great help to him with his own holdings."

Annabelle laughed. "I don't know what happened to those of us who came after Mara. The smart business gene skipped right over all of us. Mara's daughter wasn't interested in running and managing her mother's ventures so she sold off everything after her mother died."

"What did you do for work?" Lin asked the woman.

"I was a teacher. My mother was a teacher as well. And Mara's daughter became a teacher, too. Somehow the business gene got swapped out for a teaching gene." Annabelle shrugged. "We all would have done better financially if we had run our own businesses, but I guess, you can't change who you are."

"I should have been a teacher myself," Louella sighed. "I'd have a stable income and benefits if I'd gone into teaching. I should have listened to you," she said to her mother. "You always told me it was a very good profession, but I didn't pay any attention."

Annabelle gave her daughter a kind smile.

"You'll be okay. You know that you and Angela can move in with me."

Louella gave her mother a weary smile. "I appreciate it."

"How's your daughter doing?" Lin asked Louella.

"She's okay. She's in rehab right now following another surgery. I'll be heading back to the mainland the day after tomorrow." Louella went to the kitchen to refill a glass pitcher with ice water and lemons.

Annabelle's face took on a worried expression. "She told you about Angela? About her husband?"

Lin and Viv nodded.

"It was an awful shock to lose Phil. And to have Angela so severely injured is just unbelievable. Phil had the finances in a heck of a mess. Louella didn't have any idea. He did well with his law practice, but he was very overextended. He'd borrowed quite a large sum of money and was having trouble making the payments. Poor Lou has to sell this house and her home outside of Boston. Whoever thinks this sort of trouble will hit you? It's knocked us to our knees. I try to stay upbeat and positive for her. We have a long, long road ahead of us."

"We're very sorry about all of it," Lin said.

"I wasn't going to bring the accident up with you.

Louella and I are thankful for the small break we have from visiting with both of you for a little while," Annabelle said. "It's nice to be able to think and talk about something besides sadness and bills, and medical interventions, and what to do next. So if you have more to ask, I'm more than willing to keep talking."

"In doing your research, did you come upon anything that might indicate Mara and Louis Whitman might have been in a relationship?" Viv asked the woman.

Annabelle looked amused. "A relationship? Not at all. I think one marriage was enough for Mara. Like I said, she was an independent person. I get the impression that being married wasn't Mara's favorite thing. I think she was always the one in control and had no interest in romance or finding another husband."

"Do you think there was competition between her and her husband?" Lin asked.

"I'd sure bet there was. Maybe they didn't even like one another. And if Lewis Whitman had some idea to peddle about a partnership in the hotel or some other investment, I'd be surprised if Mara even gave him a meeting."

"But Whitman made the trip from the mainland

to the island," Viv said with pinched eyebrows. "Would he do that if he hadn't received some positive feedback from Mara on whatever his business idea was?"

"Maybe she met with him as a professional courtesy," Annabelle said as Louella returned to the porch with more refreshments.

"Are you talking about Lewis Whitman?" Louella asked.

"I was saying that I don't think Mara would have taken on a partner for her business ventures," Annabelle told her daughter.

"I'd agree with that," Louella nodded. "I don't know half of what my mother knows about Mara, but what I do know, would lead me to believe that Mara wouldn't give up any control and certainly wouldn't have wanted to split any profits with anyone else."

"We're on the same page," Annabelle acknowledged.

Lin accepted one of the huge chocolate chip cookies Louella offered to her and took a bite before bringing up the next question. "Viv and I were speculating. Could it be possible that the cause of the fire was arson?"

Annabelle's eyes widened. "Arson. I've wondered that myself. The investigation into the blaze was spotty at best. I think a smart person could have easily tricked the fire and police force here at the time. I think the fire most certainly could have been arson."

Viv asked, "Do you have any idea as to who might have done it and why it was done?"

Annabelle tipped her head to the side a little. "Mara?"

"You mean to get the insurance money?"

"Maybe. I don't think Mara had ever been in such a tough position before. Most of the time, her investments paid off. Not this time though. She'd just sunk a ton of money into refurbishing the place. Transportation to the hotel was about to drop off to nothing. Mara had to come up with an idea to save tourism, or she probably would have had severe financial problems."

"Much like me," Louella noted sadly.

Annabelle patted her daughter's knee, and went on. "Any solution to the transportation issue would have required a huge influx of money. I've always wondered if Mara was tired of the whole thing and considered ending her investment in the hotel by getting rid of it and collecting the insurance."

"Do you think someone else could have set the hotel on fire?"

Annabelle's eyes widened. "To what purpose?"

Louella added her own questions. "What reason would someone have to set the blaze? There were no other investors. There wasn't even another partner. Why would someone bother to burn the place down? For what advantage?"

Lin looked warily from one woman to the other. "To kill Mara?"

Annabelle's mouth dropped open. "Murder?" She blinked a few times. "Mara murdered? I never thought about that. Let me look through my information again and I'll get back to you. Maybe there's something I missed."

# 15

It was early evening when Lin and Viv headed down to the docks where John and Viv kept their boat. They walked along the brick sidewalks under the not-yet illuminated old-fashioned light posts and passed the shops and restaurants busy with the tourists and locals.

When they reached the boat and were about to go aboard, they spotted Libby walking toward them and waved to her.

"Have you been shopping?" Lin asked.

"I met a friend for an early drink and some appetizers. It's been a busy few days and we both were happy to have some time together to relax and talk. How are both of you?"

"We're going to have dinner on the boat later when John and Jeff get here," Viv explained.

"How is the new mystery coming along?"

"Slowly," Lin told her. "We've met with a couple of descendants of Mara Winslow. Viv and I have been considering whether the fire might have been set."

"Hmm." Libby nodded, not a bit surprised by the suggestion. "Murder? Or are you thinking Mara set the place on fire for the insurance money?"

"Either. Both. We haven't figured it out," Lin said.

"And the ghost? Anything new from her?"

"She's appeared in different places ... at the home of her descendant, outside the historical museum library. When we were leaving the beach the other day, I heard screams coming from the ghost-hotel."

Libby made eye contact with Lin. "Try not to allow manifestations like that to upset you. Treat them like clues or additional details that are needed to determine what the ghost wants from you. Try to consider them rationally and not emotionally."

"That can be very hard to do." Viv shook her head and gave her cousin a caring touch on her arm.

"I understand that." Libby's voice was gentle. "Just

try your best to protect your physical, mental, and emotional health. These cases can be all-consuming. Step back now and then, take time for yourself."

"I've been trying to do that," Lin said. "Jeff and I are running in the summer solstice race so we've been training a little for that."

Libby frowned. "I meant for you to do something fun, not something that tortures you."

Lin and Viv chuckled, and then Viv said to the older woman, "I'm always careful to follow your advice. I will *not* be taking part in the race."

"Smart woman." Libby patted Viv on the shoulder. "My associate who has experience with shared dreams will be coming to the island in a few days. I'd like all of us to meet with her. She'll be a valuable resource. Be sure Leonard comes as well."

Viv looked wary. "Is she going to scare us?"

Libby kept an even expression. "She isn't a frightening person."

"I mean will she tell us things that will upset or worry us?" Viv clarified.

"Information is power, Vivian. The more knowledge you have, the better. The unknown is the thing that can cause us worry. The meeting will be beneficial. Think of questions you want to ask her." Libby looked from Viv to Lin. "What about your dreams? Have they remained the same?"

The cousins both sighed.

"They've changed," Lin said. "We can see a little more of the surroundings. Nothing that tells us where we are, but we can now see a door."

Viv said, "We're surrounded by smoke and fire. Lin and I are behind the door. We can't get it open. We're screaming for Leonard to help us."

For a moment, a look of alarm passed over Libby's face before she was able to bring her expression back to neutral. "Does Leonard get you out of the room? Is he able to help you?"

"The dream ends before that point," Lin explained.

"You don't know where you are?"

Lin shook her head.

"All three of you are experiencing the same details in your dreams?"

"Yes," Viv said.

"I'll let my associate know what's happening with the nightmares," Libby assured them. "She'll be able to help."

A breeze came off the water and rustled Lin's long brown hair. The wharf was crowded now with tourists strolling by to admire the boats and yachts, and the three women had to move closer together to allow people to pass by.

"I need to get home," Libby said. "Call me if you need me. You're not alone in this. We're here to support and help you. You're doing good work." She hugged the cousins before starting on her way. "Enjoy your dinner on the boat."

Lin watched the woman walk down the dock. "I think she's getting softer as she gets older."

Viv smiled. "Libby's always been no-nonsense, but every now and then, she lets her serious side slip away and her caring side peeks out for a few seconds. She means what she says. She's always got our backs."

The cousins got settled on the boat and Viv slipped some nachos into the oven in the galley before carrying two glasses of wine to the table on the deck facing the wharf.

"If the guys don't get here soon, you and I can eat all the nachos." Viv set a glass down in front of Lin.

"I'm starving so it won't be hard for me to clean the plate." Lin took a grateful sip from her glass.

The lights from the boats and shops lining one side of the docks glittered on the water as a few ducks slid by on their way around the wharves. The air temperature still retained the day's warmth making it comfortable to sit outside in the deck chairs.

"What did you think about what Annabelle Lowell told us about Mara?" Viv asked. "She described her ancestor as independent, smart, a great businessperson. From what we've heard, do you think Mara would take on a business partner?"

"I think she'd join forces with someone if she thought she could make a good deal of money from the partnership. I think the profit would have to be very high for her to give up any control." Lin ate a few cashews from the small bowl on the table.

Viv nodded. "I agree. She sounds like someone who wanted to be the one in charge. Maybe she'd take on a partner if the deal wasn't a 50-50 split of profits. I think she'd have to have majority control in the deal."

"I think you're right," Lin said. "So was Lewis Whitman meeting Mara at the hotel to discuss a partnership?"

"Or was he there for a different reason?" Viv stood and headed for the stairs to the galley. "I'm going to bring up the nachos." She returned with the platter in one hand and her laptop in the other. "Let's see what we can find online about Mr. Whitman."

The cousins moved their chairs closer together and as they dug into the nachos, Viv tapped at her keyboard.

"Here are a few things about him. Look, here's a picture." Viv pointed.

The man had dark hair and a handlebar mustache. He was dressed in fine clothes and had an air of importance about him.

Viv summarized from one of the articles. "A well-known businessman from the time ... inherited wealth ... holdings in real estate, oil, construction, shipbuilding." She read more before sharing the information. "Shrewd, he employed questionable business practices, kept his employees' wages low, was lacking in empathy for others, swindled his partners to eliminate competition."

"Sounds like a great guy," Lin deadpanned. "Not the kind of person I'd trust to be my partner."

"Would Mara work with someone like that?" Viv narrowed her eyes.

"*Did* she work with him? Are the names of his business associates listed?" Lin questioned.

"No. No partners are listed in this article." Viv scanned two other sites, but those didn't mention the names of the people Whitman had worked with.

"Nothing. Maybe Anton can look for a connection between Mara and Whitman."

"Could there have been a falling out between them? Could they have considered a partnership to save the hotel, but it fell apart when they didn't see eye to eye? Maybe Whitman set the fire to kill Mara, but was unable to escape himself," Lin suggested as she looked out over the harbor. "Something has been picking at me about all of this. Why is Mara appearing to me now? What's going on now that has pushed her to seek help for something?"

Viv sat back in her chair. "If you can figure that out, I bet a whole bunch of stuff will become a whole lot clearer."

"Yeah. Could Lewis Whitman's descendants be doing something that Mara is angry about?"

Viv tilted her head to the side in question. "Like what?"

"I have no idea."

Adding some more nachos to her plate, Viv said, "Add that to the endless list of things Anton needs to research for us."

# 16

It was a gorgeous sunny morning as Lin, breathing hard, and with Jeff by her side, ran up the last hill of the 10k road race. They'd each struggled in places along the route, but they stayed together and encouraged one another through the tough spots. With the finish line in sight, the couple felt a burst of energy as they made their way along the road leading back toward town.

Viv, John, Anton, Libby, Leonard and Heather, and their friends, Robert Snow and his grandson, Chase, and Tim Pierce and Lori Michaels stood just before the finish cheering, whooping and hollering.

Lin and Jeff laughed and waved as they ran past the small group of well-wishers, appreciative of their support.

Crossing the finish line, the couple slowed to a walk and embraced, congratulating each other for completing the race.

"It was harder than I thought." Lin used her arm to wipe some perspiration from her forehead. "Maybe it was the humidity, or maybe I'm just slow." She smiled at her husband.

"You weren't slow at all." Jeff lifted the bottom of his sweaty t-shirt and flapped it to help cool himself down. "I had a hard time on the hill up to Cliff and the road to Madaket seemed endless. Overall, we did a good job. I'm glad we were able to finish. That finish line sure looked good to me as we were coming around the last corner."

"To me, too."

Their friends caught up to them and offered water bottles and two small dry towels.

"That was exciting." Viv handed homemade granola bars to Lin and Jeff. "I loved watching you come down the home stretch. I got some good pictures."

Ten-year-old Chase Snow gave Lin a hug. "I really like running. Maybe I can do the race with you next year."

"I'd love that," Lin told the boy. "But I might not be able to keep up with you."

Chase nodded and gave Lin a kind smile. "Don't worry. I'd wait for you."

"Very impressive, but that's not surprising," Libby praised the couple. "I'm very proud of you both."

"You made it look easy." Anton adjusted his straw hat with a wide brim, and sipped from his iced coffee. "Thankfully, I have the brains to never have tried running."

"I'm with you," Viv agreed, patting the man on the back.

Tim Pierce said, "Lori and I have been inspired. We'd like to run it next year, too."

"Maybe we can get a team together," Lori suggested. "We could raise money for a charity."

Heather's voice was excited. "I'd love to do that. Count me in."

Leonard's face clouded. "You can count me *out*. I'll coordinate the cheering section."

The friends walked back into town together to enjoy the summer solstice celebration. Food trucks parked along Main Street, a four-person band played on one corner, several side roads were closed off to traffic where an arts and crafts fair had been set up, stores had sidewalk sales going on, and the sidewalks were crowded with people strolling around.

As they walked, Lin asked Anton, “Do you know if Lewis Whitman has any descendants here on-island?”

Anton slipped his sunglasses on. “I’m not sure. I haven’t been able to look into that yet. Why do you ask?”

“Viv and I are trying to come up with the reason why Mara has chosen now to appear and ask for help.”

Anton said, “Yes. That is a missing link in the case. I’ll see what I can find out about Lewis Whitman and whether or not he has any ties to Nantucket. Are other possible reasons swirling around in your head about why the ghost has appeared now?”

Lin shrugged a shoulder. “Just that Mara’s descendant, Louella, recently lost her husband, and her daughter was seriously injured in the car accident. Louella’s bills are mounting and her husband left behind a great deal of debt. If Louella’s situation is the reason Mara has shown up now asking for assistance, I don’t know how we can help her with that problem. A ghost has never wanted something we can’t deliver. Sure, some needs are really difficult to make happen, but there's always a possibility we can achieve it for the spirit. Louella's situation can't be the reason why Mara is here. It has to be something else."

"Are you sure?" Anton questioned, raising an eyebrow.

A puzzled look washed over Lin's face. "How can we help Louella with her financial problems?" She shook her head. "I think the ghost being here might have something to do with her death in the fire. If she was murdered, she might want that to be known. She might want her killer to be publicly named."

"All that is true," Anton said. "But why is that so important to Mara *now*?"

"Because she finally found someone who can see ghosts? I just don't know."

Jeff came over to Lin and the two turned left toward Viv and John's boat so they could shower and change there and then meet back with their friends a little later.

Nicky and Queenie were sunning themselves on the deck, and they stood up and stretched lazily before greeting the couple.

While Jeff went below to shower, Lin sat in the deck chair. Her legs were already starting to get sore and she massaged her thighs and calves to relieve the tightness gathering in the muscles. She was feeling low energy and was looking forward to eating lunch with her friends.

As Lin leaned back in her chair, the warmth of the sun felt so good that she closed her eyes to rest until Jeff was done with his shower ... and in just a few minutes, she had dozed off ... and not long afterwards, the nightmare started.

Lin was surrounded by darkness so thick that she couldn't see a thing. Holding her arms out in front of her trying to feel for something solid, her feet were as heavy as cement blocks. She trudged slowly forward. The smell of smoke was overpowering. She called for someone, but later, she wouldn't remember who she was calling to. When her hand touched something, she ran her fingers over the wood. It was a heavy door and it was warm under her hand.

Using her sense of touch, she fumbled for the doorknob, but when she found it and turned the knob, the door wouldn't open. She used her shoulder to push against it, but it wouldn't budge.

Still unable to see, anxiety flooded her body and fear threatened to swallow her up. Tears gathered in her eyes. She called out. "Open the door! I need to open this door. Hurry!"

Once again, Lin bashed her shoulder into the door, but it remained closed. She pounded on the wood with both hands. "Let me in. Open this door," she screamed.

Her energy sapped, and coughing from the all the smoke, she slipped to her knees. *I don't know what to do.*

Leaning her hand against the door, the wood was so hot that she pulled it back.

And then to her surprise, the door creaked open and Lin's head snapped up. Lacking the strength to stand, she crawled on her hands and knees into the room.

Feeling her way around, she slowly inched forward. Surrounded by darkness and smoke, it was still impossible to see. She called out again, but was met with silence.

Suddenly, part of the smoke cleared for a moment, and in those few seconds, she spotted a woman lying on the floor, unconscious. *Mara Winslow?*

When Lin woke with a start and almost tumbled from her chair, Nicky rushed to her side and licked her hand.

Looking around to reorient herself, she blinked and coughed. "I'm okay, Nick. I fell asleep."

Reaching to pat the dog, her hand hurt and she pulled it back. Turning it over, she saw that the palm of her right hand looked sunburnt.

Jeff came up to the deck. "I'm all done. Your turn. Is something wrong with your hand?"

Lin held it out for her husband to see.

Holding Lin's hand gently in his, he asked, "Did you touch something hot? It looks like a slight burn."

"Jeff."

When her husband glanced up and saw the look in her eyes, his face fell. "What happened?"

"I dozed off while you were below." Lin coughed again and then swallowed hard before telling him about her dream. "I touched a door. If felt so hot, I pulled my hand back." She looked down at the pink skin on her palm. "I touched the door with this hand." When she made eye contact with him again, her face wore a dumbfounded look. "How can this be? I burned my hand in a dream?"

Jeff knelt in front of her and wrapped her in a hug. "I don't know," he whispered, trying to process what she'd told him. He leaned back. "Is it possible that the dream was so real, that your brain sent signals to the nerves that you'd burned yourself? And then the skin turned pink in response?"

Lin didn't know what to say.

Jeff stood. "I'll get a cool cloth for your hand." He hurried down the steps to the galley where he got a face cloth, wet it, and brought it up to Lin. "Here, this will make it feel better. I bet the skin will be back to normal in a few minutes."

Lin clenched the cold cloth in her fist. "Do you really think that's what happened? The dream made my brain think it was real?"

"It seems possible, doesn't it?"

With a tired smile, Lin said, "I guess. A lot of things that go on around us would seem impossible to most people so maybe what happened to my hand really is the result of my brain believing a dream actually happened." She moved the cloth and looked at her palm. "It feels better already."

"Good." Jeff placed his hand on her shoulder and cheerfully kidded, "You never cease to amaze me. There's no end to the things you can do."

Still staring at her pink hand, Lin grumped. "But why do they always have to be such weird things?"

# 17

Lin, Viv, and Libby stood on the corner of South Beach Street and Broad Street speaking together in hushed tones. Viv held her cousin's hand palm-up inspecting the pink skin that looked like it had been burned from touching a hot pan in the oven.

Libby took a few glances at the hand while thinking over what Lin had told them about nodding off in the deck chair on Viv and John's boat.

"It's most likely the result of the power of your imagination," the older woman pointed out. "The mind is a powerful thing. Your brain sent a message to the nerves and the skin on the hand flushed due to the dream."

"I prefer to call it a nightmare," Viv said still cradling Lin's hand in hers. "What will happen next?

One of us will fall in the dream and we'll wake up with a broken leg?"

Libby gave Viv the side-eye. "I think that would be more difficult to pull off than tinging the skin red."

"It must have been a very vivid dream." Viv gently released the hand. "Was I in it?"

"I didn't see you in it, but I feel like you were there with me." Lin took a deep breath and straightened her shoulders. "The dream and the road race have sapped my energy."

"What about some ice cream?" Viv asked. "How about a chocolate milkshake with whipped cream on top?"

A little smile spread over Lin's lips. "That actually sounds really good."

"And how about a grilled cheese sandwich from Stubby's to go along with the shake? Your body needs to recover from the road race."

Lin chuckled. "That sounds good, too."

"I'll leave you to gorge on those items," Libby said. "I'm going to find Anton. We're going to have a nice, civilized sit-down lunch by the water. I'm also going to contact my associate and tell her what happened during your nightmare," she told Lin. "My friend should have as much information as possible before meeting us to discuss the shared dreams." Libby hugged the cousins and started away to locate Anton. "I'm sure we'll run into you later today before the festival is over."

When Viv and Lin headed to the Juice Bar ice cream shop to stand in line, Viv looked into her cousin's eyes. "Are you upset about your hand? I don't mean your hand ... I mean what happened to cause it."

Lin asked, "What do you think caused it? My mind influencing my neurons or whatever that means?"

"I guess that's possible."

"But what?"

"But you were in a fire and a smoke-filled room and you were trying to get out," Viv said. "I know you weren't physically in the room." She struggled with how to say it. "But was your spirit in the room?"

Lin turned to face her cousin. "My spirit?"

"Like what the ghosts are made of. The part of them that makes them who they are. They leave their physical bodies behind, but they're still present ... they're still themselves. I don't know what else to call it. You know what I mean."

"Yeah, I do. So what are you thinking? My spirit

left me for a while and actually was in the room I was dreaming about?"

"That sounds really, really nuts. My crazy suggestion is more outlandish than being able to see ghosts." Viv pushed her light brown hair from her eyes as they stepped forward in the ice cream line. "Forget I said anything. It's ridiculous."

"Is it?"

"My brain can't handle this stuff." Viv took a deep breath. "Let's get our ice cream and stop thinking about it for a while. We need some time off and I have to go back to the bookstore in two hours to relieve Mallory." She eyed Lin. "Unless you need to talk about it."

"I'm okay. There aren't any answers anyway. I think an afternoon off is a good idea."

They got their ice creams and their grilled cheese sandwiches, and after scarfing down the food, they walked around the festival until they met up again with their friends, and John and Jeff. They all walked around the street fair, listened to a band for a while, checked out the sidewalk sales, and then got lemonades and sat in a small park to relax in the shade.

Leonard sat next to Lin. "I recall a summer festival not so long ago when you found me drunk as a skunk down by the docks." For years after losing his wife, Leonard would go off the rails around the anniversary of her death almost drowning in a sea of misery.

Lin smiled at the memory. "I remember."

"You didn't know me all that well, but you and Jeff took me home so I wouldn't get into trouble being drunk in a public place. You told me that Marguerite would want me to be happy. You were kind to me, Coffin."

Lin nodded shyly. "You were worth the trouble."

"If it wasn't for you, I probably wouldn't have made it. Your friendship brought me back to life."

Shifting on the bench so she faced the man, she looked into his face. "You *would* have made it. You're strong. But I know both of our lives are better because of our friendship. And I don't want to lose that. So you'd better be strong when whatever's coming, comes our way." Lin's eyes moistened. "Because I don't think we'll be able to get out of it without you."

"I'll be ready. I won't let anything happen to you." Leonard's jaw muscle twitched. "Something bad will happen ... only over my dead body."

~

Back at home with Jeff and Nicky, Lin and her husband made dinner, they sat out on the deck for a while, and then headed to bed where Jeff read a thriller novel, Lin worked on her crossword puzzle book, and Nicky snoozed, squished in between them.

After turning off the light, Lin ended up tossing and turning, and afraid of waking Jeff, she got up, pulled on a sweatshirt, and carried a glass of water out to the deck.

Nicky came out through the doggy door and lay down at Lin's feet where he sniffed the night air. Lin leaned back in her Adirondack chair and looked up at the stars. The sky looked beautiful, and staring into space helped calm her.

There was too much going on and she didn't understand much of it. It was taking too long to figure things out. There were pieces to the puzzle in her grasp, but they weren't enough to make anything clear.

"How will I get the information I need, Nick?"

The dog stretched his neck and nuzzled at Lin's fingertips.

"My palm is almost all better. There's just a little streak of pink left." With a sigh, she asked, "What was that all about?"

A whoosh of cold air enveloped the young woman, and she shifted her eyes out to the field. In a moment, the ghost materialized, the red light still emanating from her. She stood still and silent, looking over at Lin.

Nicky wagged his tail at the spirit.

They stayed that way for a quite a while, with the ghost and Lin gazing at one another.

Lin didn't speak aloud, but said the words in her mind. *I'm stuck. I don't know if I'm on the right track. I don't know how to help you. I'm not sure what you want me to do.*

The ghost just stared back, her expression neutral.

*I think what we see in our dreams is going to happen soon. I can feel it getting closer. But why? What are we supposed to do? What do you need? Why are you showing up now? What am I missing?*

The spirit nodded in an encouraging way.

*Can you help me figure it out? Can you lead me in the right direction? I'm not sure what to do.*

A kind smile formed on the ghost-woman's face, and then the shimmering atoms that made up her form began to swirl, faster and faster, until they blurred, and with a spark she was gone.

Lin's shoulders drooped. "I thought she might give me a clue," she told the dog.

The kitchen door opened. "Lin? Are you okay?" Jeff stepped outside onto the deck.

"I couldn't sleep so I came out here for a while. I had a visitor again."

Even though he couldn't see ghosts, Jeff glanced round the yard. "Mara?"

"At least that's who I think the ghost is." Lin nodded. "She stood in the field and stared at me. I was hoping for a detail … or something."

Jeff took the chair next to his wife. "Nothing though?"

"No."

"Maybe your dreams will lead you. Maybe some more time has to pass."

"Maybe." Lin reached for his hand and gave it a squeeze.

"Is your hand feeling better?"

"It is. The pink is almost gone."

"Do you want to talk about it?" Jeff asked.

"I guess not. I don't know what to say or ask."

"I wish I could do something to help."

Lin smiled. "You do help, just by being you."

"It'll be okay."

"Are you sure?"

"Yes. Remember what Sebastian and Emily told you. *When the time comes, don't be afraid.* It will all work out the way it's supposed to."

Lin reached up for her horseshoe necklace and rubbed it between her fingers. "We're going to talk with Libby's friend in a few days. The one who knows about shared dreams."

"That will be really helpful," Jeff told her. "She'll be able to answer your questions. Things will become clearer. She'll help you understand what's going on."

"She'll help with our understanding about how shared dreams work," Lin said. "But I don't know how to figure out what Mara wants from us. And this woman won't be able to help with that."

"Every step will lead you in the right direction," Jeff said. "You'll find what you need to find, and you'll be where you need to be."

Lin gave his hand another squeeze, looked out over the yard to the spot where Mara had stood, and hoped with all her heart that Jeff was right.

# 18

Lin and Leonard met with a new client to go over the project the homeowners had in mind. The house had recently been renovated and although the result was beautiful, the yard and gardens had been left in ruin.

The landscapers, along with Nicky, walked the property with the couple to show them where garden beds and features would be located. Lin and Leonard had already gone over the hard copies of the proposal on a laptop which included mock-ups of how everything would look once it was completed, but they thought it was important to bring the owners outside for a walkthrough to be sure everything fit properly into their intended use of the land.

"This is where the pergola will be placed and garden beds will be on three sides. A variety of climbing vines will be trained up the sides of the structure to provide the sense of a cozy, private space."

Lin and Leonard took turns explaining where a water feature would be placed, where gardens would be located, and what kinds of plants would be included in them. They strolled around the yard showing the placement of brick and stone walkways while at the same time, pulling up the mock-up images on a tablet.

The homeowners asked good questions and were more than satisfied with the answers, and they signed the contract while standing in the spot where a new water feature was planned. The couple shook hands with the landscapers and patted the dog on the head, all the while praising the friendly, well-behaved animal.

Back in the truck, Leonard said, "The cur got more praise than we did."

Lin chuckled and turned the truck onto the road. "That's why we bring Nick along. He's our secret weapon in convincing new clients to hire us. Who can resist an adorable dog?"

Leonard patted the dog sitting next to him on the

passenger seat. "Next, he'll be wanting a cut of the profits."

"Hmm, he hadn't thought of that ... until now." Lin smiled at her friend.

The partners had worked at different locations all day until Lin picked up Leonard to present the landscaping plan to the new clients.

"I haven't told you what happened to me at the festival."

With narrowed eyes, the man quickly turned his head to look at Lin. "What now?"

She explained dozing off on John's boat, dreaming of being in a dark room with smoke and fire, and waking up disoriented ... with what seemed like a burn on the palm of her hand.

Leonard's eyes were pinned on the young woman driving the truck.

After a few seconds passed, Lin took a glance at him. "Are you going to say anything?"

"I don't know what the heck to say. What in the world?"

"I know. It's baffling." She told him the two explanations she, Libby, and Viv had come up with.

"So your brain might have thought what happened to you was real and then sent signals to your nerves which then caused the skin on your palm to turn red as if it really *did* get burned."

"That's right." Lin took a tight turn onto a side road.

Leonard cocked his head to the side. "Really? That can happen?"

"I don't know. But something caused my skin to redden."

"Maybe you had a reaction to being all hot and sweaty from the road race." Leonard scrambled for a simple explanation. "You know ... some people get hives from heat or something they ate or whatever. Your skin might have reacted to some irritant and got all pink."

"That's a good idea," Lin told him. "Now there are three possibilities. My brain caused it from the dream experience, I had a reaction to the heat, and the idea Viv came up with."

Leonard shook his head. "I don't get Viv's idea. Well, I guess I get it, since I was able to see Marguerite's ghost. But I thought you had to be dead before your spirit went wandering off on its own."

A smile crept over Lin's mouth. "Maybe you don't have to be. Maybe in some circumstances, the spirit can leave, do something it has to do, and come back."

With a sigh, Leonard looked out the window at the passing scenery. "Why can't we just have normal lives?"

"Think of all the excitement we'd miss."

Nicky let out a soft yip of agreement.

"You know how at the festival you told me that our friendship made our lives better?" Leonard asked. "I'm re-thinking that idea."

Lin laughed at the comment as she brought the truck to a stop in front of Leonard's house, and before he got out, she asked, "Which of the three theories do you think is the correct one?"

Giving Nicky a pat goodbye and opening the passenger side door, he said, "I'm waiting for theory number four before making a decision. Have a nice evening, Coffin. I'll see you bright and early tomorrow morning." And with that, he shut the door and headed for his house.

Wanting a break from routine, Lin and Jeff strolled along the brick walkways from their house into town heading out for dinner at a barbecue restaurant they liked. They talked about their workdays with Lin telling him that she and Leonard had secured a great new project and Jeff describing the house renovation job on Martha's Vineyard he and Kurt had landed.

"Things are looking terrific for our businesses." Jeff beamed as he and Lin walked hand-in-hand toward the docks.

"We're sure going to be busy," Lin said. "But it's a good kind of busy. We're lucky we have so many clients."

"I think this partnership with Kurt is going to be really profitable. I'm excited about the future."

After being seated at a cozy table at the back of the restaurant, they sipped their drinks while looking over the menu even though they always ordered the same things ... the roasted mushroom roll with lemon aioli for Lin and the pulled pork sandwich for Jeff.

"What are you going to get?" Jeff asked with a grin knowing very well what Lin would order.

"The usual. You?"

"The same as always. I don't know why we even bother to look at the choices."

After dinner, the couple planned to browse in some of the shops and then head to a pub where Viv and John's band would be playing that night.

"I need a new briefcase," Jeff said. "The one I

have is ratty looking and I want to look professional and successful when I meet with clients."

Lin suggested one of the stores off Main Street where she'd recently shopped. "I saw a few nice looking briefcases in there."

"Let's check it out before we go to the pub."

The meals arrived and the food was as delicious as always.

Lin wiped a little sauce from her lip. "Viv and I have another meeting tomorrow with Annabelle Lowell, Mara's great-granddaughter. She called and asked if we could come by. She only said she had a couple of things to share with us."

Jeff's face brightened. "That's good news. She might give you some information that leads you in a new direction."

"I hope so. At this point, any little thing would be a help."

When they'd finished dinner, they walked around the town past shops and eateries, with the growing darkness interrupted by the golden glow of the streetlamps. The couple decided to get ice cream cones and ate them sitting on a bench overlooking the water before heading to the store that Lin had suggested to shop for briefcases.

Jeff looked over the inventory of leather goods,

narrowing it down to three different styles. He checked them out while Lin wandered around looking at other items. When they'd entered the store, a strange sensation of unease had come over her, and she'd looked around to see if a ghost was preparing to materialize, but saw nothing.

Now as she meandered around the shop waiting for Jeff to pick out a briefcase, the feeling of dread washed over her again. She stood where she was and slowly pivoted, searching for the cause of the anxiety.

People browsed the goods, the shopkeeper helped a customer with something, and a clerk brought out a few new items to place on the shelves. Everything seemed normal, nothing was wrong.

Lin walked slowly back to where Jeff was still trying to make a decision. She picked up some wallets and a passport cover to look over, and when she turned around, she spotted three other brief-cases displayed on a round table. One was made of leather, one was created from fabric, and the third was formed from metal.

Running her hand over each one, little zips of electricity sparked at her fingers when she touched the silver, metal case, and she pulled her hand back from it.

She stared at the case for a few seconds and then reached out to place her hand on it again. The sparks bit at her skin, but because she was expecting it, she didn't pull back.

Despite the uncomfortable sensation in her hands, she opened the case and inspected the interior compartments and pockets. Something about the case drew her to it.

Lin closed the briefcase with a snap and set it down on the table, but kept her hand touching the side of the metal.

A flash popped in her brain, then another. An image took form. A dark room. The smell of smoke. Then nothing. Her eyes only saw the shop she was standing in. Another light flashed in her mind. She could see flames. She was standing in front of a door. Turning the knob, she pushed it open. Lin could barely make it out ... but a woman's body lay on the floor in a smoky room. The image blurred, disappeared, then returned. Just as the vision was blurring again, Lin spotted something on the floor beside the woman.

A silver metal briefcase.

With a sudden flash of light, the vision was over.

With a slight gasp, Lin took a step back from the case on display.

Jeff came over to her carrying a soft, dark brown briefcase. "I think I like this one the best." He didn't notice his wife's odd expression. "Oh, I didn't see these on this table. Metal, huh?" Opening the silver case, he checked out the pockets, closed it, and grasping the handle, held it by his side before returning it to the table.

"I like the brown one better. I'm going to get it. Ready to go?"

"Yeah. That's a nice one." Lin forced a smile, still stunned by her vision.

As they walked to the checkout counter, she glanced over her shoulder at the metal case ... and an icy cold shiver raced down her arms.

# 19

On the drive to Louella's house to see Annabelle, Viv took a quick look at her cousin after Lin told her what happened the previous evening while shopping with Jeff for a briefcase.

"A metal briefcase set off that vision? What does it mean?"

Lin shrugged. "As usual, I have no idea. The metal briefcase in the store looked very similar to the case next to the woman on the floor. At least, it's another detail we didn't have before."

"Could you see who the woman was?"

"No, her face is always hidden from view. I don't know who it is, but it's probably Mara or her friend, Paulette."

Viv took the turn past the high school. "An interesting question would be ... what's in the case?"

"It must be relevant to our ghost in some way," Lin said. "Could the case in my vision belong to one of the women? Or maybe to Lewis Whitman? Is the metal briefcase a clue to why the old hotel burned down?"

"I wonder if I'll dream about the case tonight." Viv pulled her Jeep to stop in front of Louella's home and they got out, walked to the door, and rang the bell.

Annabelle hurried around to the front of the house from the back. "Hello there," she called. "I was in the back weeding the flower beds. The time got away from me. Come in."

The three women went into the pretty house and after Annabelle washed her hands and brought out some drinks and cookies, they all took seats in the comfortable living room.

"Will Louella be joining us?" Lin asked.

"I'm afraid not. She went back to the mainland. She has a million things to do and she didn't want to leave Angela at the rehab hospital for too long so she headed back. I'm staying to pack things up for her."

"It's too bad she has to sell the house," Viv said.

"It sure is. She loves this place, but there are more pressing needs right now. My sweet daughter has a long road ahead of her. And poor Angela. I can't stop thinking about her. I'll help them both as much as I can. I worry about Lou. She has so much worry pressing down on her."

"Any bites on the house?"

"Not yet, but I think it will sell quickly. It isn't a huge place, but it has a good location and it's a nice home. I hope someone will snap it up fast so it will be one less thing Lou has to be concerned about," Annabelle said.

"We hope so," Viv told the woman. "Anything to make things easier on Louella."

Annabelle thanked the cousins for their concern. "I got to thinking about Mara Winslow after we met last time. I spent some time thinking about her death, and considered the possibility of murder. I decided that I can't rule it out. Why someone would want to kill her though, I just don't know. I went through some of my notes and research. A good deal of it is kept on my laptop. I started rereading old letters and articles looking specifically for anything indicating trouble between Mara and someone else. I couldn't find anything suspicious or that led me to believe someone wanted her dead. That doesn't mean there wasn't someone with that intention. I just haven't found anything. It's an interesting theory and it deserves more attention."

"Do you know anything about the friendship between Mara and Paulette?" Lin asked. "Could they have had a falling out? Could Paulette have been behind the fire?"

Annabelle shook her head. "I don't think so. I think they were friends to the end. I did find a letter from Paulette to Mara mentioning the hotel and stating that things would eventually work out. I don't know if there were other letters between them discussing things in detail, but it sounded like Paulette knew about the issues with the hotel and had heard about possible plans to keep it going. She sounded like she was giving Mara encouragement."

"So maybe Mara confided in Paulette about things," Lin suggested.

"I think she did."

"I keep coming back to Lewis Whitman," Lin told the woman. "Viv and I found some articles that described Whitman in not very rosy terms."

"It seems Mr. Whitman wasn't that ethical in his business dealings," Viv added.

"Well, that's very interesting." Annabelle tapped her cheek with her index finger. "Why was he here on the island when the fire broke out? Was he at the hotel to discuss business with my great-grandmother? I wonder how he and his ideas were received."

"I guess we'll never know," Lin said. "But if Whitman attempted to do business with your great-grandmother, there might be some records somewhere."

"There could be some details in letters to friends or investors, maybe," Annabelle said. "I don't think their joint venture would have been at the point where plans were recorded or registered with the town, so that's a dead end."

"Do you have any pictures of Mara?" Viv asked. "We've only seen one of her."

Annabelle smiled. "I have a few images of her, but they aren't on this laptop. They're at my house in Somerville. I could have a close friend send them to me and when they arrive I can send them on to you, if you'll give me your email."

Lin wrote down her email address for Annabelle. "That would be great. We'd love to see more photographs of her."

"I have something for you." Annabelle handed a small piece of paper to Lin. "Since I'm the nosy type and I love genealogy, I did a little digging."

Lin had no idea what the woman was going to tell them.

"I looked for descendants of Paulette Simons, and guess what? One of her descendants is living on Cape Cod, in Chatham. That's his contact information on the paper I gave you. If you reach out to him, maybe he can tell you some things about Paulette, or point you to someone who can."

"Thank you so much," Lin told her. "I'll give him a call tomorrow."

Annabelle said, "I'll see what I can find out about Lewis Whitman, and if he and my great-grandmother had a business arrangement. It will be a break for me from packing up this house."

"Can we help you with the packing?" Viv asked.

"We'd be glad to give you a hand," Lin nodded.

With a warm smile, Annabelle said, "Oh, no. You're too kind. It's something I have to do ... some things have to be saved, some things tossed out. Lou told me what needed to be done before she left for home. And anyway, it gives me a purpose and makes me happy to help my daughter and grandchild. But I thank you for the offer. If anything comes up that I could use your help for, I'll give a yell."

Back in the Jeep, Viv said, "Annabelle is a very nice person. I wish there was something we could do for them."

"Maybe what Mara needs us to do will be beneficial to Annabelle and her family. I don't know how, but it sure would be great if it ended up that way."

Viv turned the Jeep toward town. "I'm not looking forward to meeting that associate of Libby's. What on earth is she going to tell us about shared dreams? Do you think she'll be some kind of a nut?"

"No more nutty than we are." Lin grinned.

"I'm serious. Will we be able to learn anything from her? Will she ask us a bunch of questions about our dreams? Do we want to tell her everything from them or should we hold back some information? Can we trust her?"

"Libby trusts her. That's all we have to go on. If you don't feel comfortable discussing your dreams with her, then don't share everything. She's supposed to be helping us."

"Are you uneasy about it?"

Lin said, "Yeah. It's like nothing else we've ever experienced before. I'll listen and ask questions. If she's too pushy or isn't helpful, then we'll end the meeting."

"Okay. That makes me feel better. I didn't want to feel like some unusual specimen being poked and questioned and analyzed." Viv stopped at a red light. "What about this descendant of Paulette? Will you call him?"

"Yeah, I will. What do you think about a day trip to Chatham, if he has anything to tell us?"

Viv nodded. "I like Chatham. Of course, I'll go with you. I'll do just about anything to find some information that will solve this thing. I can't wait for these nightmares to end."

"Me, too. And I know for sure, Leonard feels the same way."

"Do you think the photos of Mara that Annabelle has will be helpful to us?" Viv stopped the Jeep in front of Lin's cottage.

"They can't hurt. I was hoping to see a photo of Mara taken at the hotel. That reminds me. We should ask Anton if he ever found a layout of the hotel. I'd like to see that, if one exists."

Viv's face clouded. "If he found a diagram of the

layout, I have the feeling we'd better hurry up and see it."

Lin made eye contact with her cousin. "You think so?"

Viv nodded. "I think it's important for some reason."

Lin's shoulders sagged. "So do I."

# 20

The ferry ride from Nantucket to the mainland was smooth and enjoyable. For the entire fifty-minute ride, Lin and Viv stood in the sun on the open deck with the wind whipping their hair around their faces.

They had to raise their voices a little to be heard.

"Anton hasn't found a schematic of the hotel layout. There probably isn't one so we'll have to give up on seeing where things were located in the place," Lin said. "Anton told me he's making a crude drawing from old pictures of the hotel noting where doors and windows were placed, and from that, he's trying to guess where bedrooms and public areas were located."

"He's really a huge help to us," Viv said. "He goes above and beyond whenever we need something."

"We're lucky to know him. He's a font of knowledge."

Viv smiled. "And he's very easy to tease."

When the ferry arrived in Hyannis, the cousins disembarked and went to the car rental place to pick up their reserved vehicle, and then headed out to make the half-hour drive to Chatham.

The town of Chatham, set at the southeastern end of Cape Cod on the "elbow" of Massachusetts was first settled by the English, but the area was initially the home of the Nauset Native American tribe. Now, the town was home to a pretty main street, a lighthouse, sandy beaches, ponds, and harbors.

The cousins enjoyed the scenery as they made their way to their destination and upon arriving at Andrew Paten's home, their eyes widened. Located across from the ocean, Paten's home was surrounded by tall, green hedges affording the place a good deal of privacy. A long brick and cobblestone driveway led to a gray-shingled expanded Cape-style home of about five-thousand square feet. Flowers bloomed in beds, urns, and pots.

"Well," Viv said taking in the huge home. "I wasn't expecting this."

"Neither was I." Lin stepped out onto the driveway. "Mr. Paten must do very well."

A tall, slender man with blond hair who looked to be in his early forties stepped onto the porch with a woman who matched his appearance in physical build and hair color.

The man waved. "Hello. I'm Andrew Paten and this is my sister, Suzanne Paten-Smith."

Lin and Viv introduced themselves and handshakes went all around.

Paten said, "I asked my sister to join us. She knows far more about the family and our ancestors than I do. Please come in."

The cousins were led through a foyer down a long hallway with a living room and dining room off the hall, into a large family room with windows on three sides that looked out over the perfect lawn and beyond to the sea.

"What a lovely home," Viv told the man after they all took comfortable seats by one of the big windows.

The coffee table had beverages, a plate of crackers and cheese, and another platter with cut-up fruit and veggies. Small white plates and linen napkins sat next to the refreshments.

Lin and Viv explained their interest in Paulette Simons and her connection to Mara Winslow, and to the old hotel on Nantucket. They talked about their early ancestors dating back centuries to the first settlers on the island.

"I found a booklet my grandfather had saved put out by the historical commission about old homes and buildings on Nantucket. There was a picture and a blurb about the hotel and it got me interested in its history," Lin explained.

"One thing led to another," Viv said, "and we found out about Mara and Paulette and that they both died in the blaze that burned part of the hotel to the ground. We've learned a little about Mara, but we don't know much at all about Paulette. They both seemed like very independent women."

Suzanne nodded. "I'd agree with that. I think they were strong women who made the most of their intelligence and their desire to make something of themselves. They both wanted to earn a living in order to take care of themselves and their loved ones."

"We didn't know Paulette had children," Viv told

them. "Obviously, she did since I'm sitting across from her descendants."

Andrew said, "Paulette had twin boys. Her husband died when he was around thirty."

"It was a lucky thing she'd been trained as a nurse so she could provide for her family. Her mother lived with them and took care of the children while Paulette worked," Suzanne said. "It was a very good arrangement that benefitted Paulette, her mother, and the boys."

"How old were the boys when Paulette died?" Lin asked.

"They were ten years old," Suzanne said. "They lived with the grandmother until they went off to college. Paulette had been a saver and had put away money since her early twenties."

"How do you know all of this?" Lin questioned.

"Paulette kept a diary and it has been passed down over the years. I was intrigued with it since I was a little girl so my mother gave it to me."

"The diary must give a good deal of information about a woman living, working, and raising a family at the turn of the century," Lin guessed.

"It's a very personal account, but it doesn't tell much about Paulette's thoughts. She made to-do lists in the pages, noted doctor's appointments for the children, talked about illnesses they experienced, doing shopping, and about her medical experiences as a nurse. She died before the 1918 Spanish flu. It would have been very interesting to read what she would have written if she'd lived during that time," Suzanne said.

With a smile Viv asked, "Have any of Paulette's descendants followed in her footsteps and entered the medical profession?"

Andrew and Suzanne shared a smile, and he said, "Quite a few family members have gone into medicine ... nurses, doctors, dentists. We cover just about all the bases. I started and run a medical supply business and Suzanne is an emergency room physician."

"It seems to run in the blood," Suzanne nodded.

"Do you know anything about the friendship between Paulette and Mara?" Lin asked.

"A little. Do you know how they met?" Suzanne asked.

Lin said, "It was because Mara had fallen and broken an ankle and needed a nurse for a while. Paulette was the nurse Mara hired. Is that right?"

Suzanne nodded. "Yes, that was the beginning of the friendship. It was a surprising pairing in some ways. Mara was a high-powered businesswoman and

Paulette was a nurse. They lived in two different worlds and it wouldn't seem they'd have much in common. But in reality, the women were very much alike. Both wanted to work and be financially secure, both lost their husbands early in their marriages, both had young children to care for and support, both were smart, hardworking, and forward-thinking."

"They were impressive women," Lin said. "No wonder they struck up a friendship."

"Do you know anything about a man named Lewis Whitman?" Viv questioned. "Was his name mentioned in Paulette's diary?"

Suzanne looked surprised by the question. "How do you know the name?"

Lin explained, "He was the third person who died in the hotel fire. We wondered if he was connected in any way to Paulette or Mara."

"Whitman hired Paulette for a short time to tend to one of his little boys. She made it clear in her writings that she did not like the man," Suzanne said.

"What did she say about him?" Lin was excited to hear of the connection between the two people.

Andrew spoke up. "I know the answer to this question. Whitman was greedy, sneaky, unethical, and had a boasting, overbearing attitude. Paulette wrote about how unpleasant the man was … demanding, domineering, treating her as if she knew nothing."

"And she decided to quit the job and gave her two-week notice," Suzanne added.

"Did Mara know Whitman?" Viv asked.

"I assume they knew each other because they were prominent people in business circles at the time," Andrew said as he looked to his sister for her opinion.

"I'd guess they knew each other for the same reason. I don't recall anything in Paulette's diary mentioning Whitman and Mara in the same entry."

"Does Paulette talk about visiting Nantucket in her diary?" Viv asked the brother and sister.

"She made a couple of mentions about it. I remember she made an entry about going with Mara to see the hotel she'd purchased. Paulette didn't make longwinded accounts. She almost used the diary as a schedule. She'd write *doctor's appointment* or she'd make entries about where she was working on certain days. Sometimes she'd write a comment about the day or a patient she was seeing or that she spent the afternoon at the park. It was those kinds of things. How I would have loved it if she'd written long passages about her daily experiences. I suppose she didn't have time for that sort of thing." Suzanne looked from Viv to Lin. "I have a few photographs of Paulette. Would you like to see them?"

Lin almost jumped out of her skin. "Oh, yes, we'd love to."

Suzanne stood and went to a desk in the corner of the room where she picked up a leather folder and carried it back to her seat. "When Andrew asked me to come to meet with you, I thought I'd bring the photos. I left the diary at home as it only has the short entries. I didn't think that was worth your time, but pictures are a wonderful link to the past." She spread a few photos on the table. "This was taken at Paulette's graduation from nursing school. This one shows Paulette with her husband, her mother, and her twin boys."

Lin and Viv leaned forward to have a look.

"Here's Paulette with a friend. I don't know the person's name." Suzanne said to herself, "Where's the fourth one?" She opened the folder again. "Oh, here it is. This one is of Paulette and Mara."

Lin and Viv perked right up as the woman placed it on the table.

Paulette was wearing her nurse's uniform and stood next to Mara who had on a lovely dress. They must have been in Mara's home. The furnishings in the background looked expensive and well-chosen. The women were smiling as if they'd shared a private joke.

Lin smiled while she looked at the old photograph. It was clear the women were friends and were comfortable with one another.

About to lean back, Lin saw something on the table behind the women in the photograph that sent a chill down her back and her heart rate racing.

On the table was an open metal briefcase, very similar to the one in the shop where Jeff had bought his case and exactly like the one she saw in her vision of the woman lying on the floor in the smoke-filled room.

*The woman on the floor in that room has to be Mara.*

# 21

"The idea of shared dreaming or mutual dreaming has been around for centuries, probably for thousands of years." In her mid-fifties, Simone Williams was of medium height and moved like a trained dancer. Her straight, black hair reached her shoulders and her eyes were a bright, intense blue. The woman had a calm, approachable presence and the four people in the room listened intently to her.

Lin, Viv, Leonard, and Libby sat on cushioned chairs and sofas on the back covered porch of Libby's farmhouse looking out over rolling green fields. It was a warm, sunny day and everyone was comfortable sipping cold drinks in the beautiful setting.

"I'll tell you a bit about shared dreams," Simone

said. "You may stop me at any point to ask questions, and then at the end, we can talk about your own experiences. If you don't want to share your dreams, that's perfectly okay. I'm here to help you in whatever way I can. I won't pressure you or ask a million questions. I won't put you on the spot. Relax, listen, accept what you want to accept, and reject what you don't feel comfortable with. No one has all the answers. We're all learning as we go."

Lin liked the woman immediately upon meeting her. Her friendly, gentle manner put everyone at ease.

"I'll give you my background to start off." Simone held a glass of water in her hand and took a drink from it before setting it on the glass coffee table. "I grew up in Oregon in a family of five. My parents were artists and educators. They had open minds and encouraged that same characteristic in us. I went to college in California and studied anthropology. I went on for graduate degrees and completed my doctorate in counseling psychology. I teach at the college level, have my own private practice, I write, and give lectures around the world. The members of our family often experienced shared dreaming. Mutual dreams are most often shared between people with very close relationships ... spouses, children, other family members, dear friends. Dreams can be shared among strangers, but only if those people have very strong mutual goals."

Lin interrupted. "What sort of mutual goals?"

"For instance, there are groups of people who purposely dream together for things like peace, or a healthier world. It's believed that sharing hopes for the future can make those goals come about."

"That's really interesting," Viv nodded.

"There is very little research on shared dreams and it will be enlightening when more study on the phenomenon is undertaken. For now, we exchange information with one another and try to make sense of it as best we can," Simone said. "Meshing is a term used to describe people having different dreams, but with very similar elements in them. Same dreams or meeting dreams are those where people meet and communicate within the same dream. You might ask, how is that possible? Theories include telepathy and alternate realities. People may communicate via mental telepathy or they may actually enter an alternate reality where they can actually interact with one another. Perhaps, the dream world is a form of different reality."

Leonard's face took on a skeptical expression and Simone noticed.

"I understand that what I'm saying is considered unbelievable, impossible, or ridiculous. However, many things have been viewed that way over thousands of years of human experience, and many of those things that were scoffed at have become reality."

Simone looked at the people across from her and smiled. "You probably have a million questions for me. Shall we go ahead and discuss?"

Viv shook her head. "I don't even know where to start."

With a frown, Leonard asked, "Can we get hurt in our dreams?"

Simone didn't reply for several moments, taking her time to gather her thoughts. "There have been instances when people have suffered injuries related to mutual dreaming. It's rare, but it has happened."

Leonard passed his hand over his face. "So it can be dangerous in some circumstances."

Simone gave a nod. "It's possible, yes."

Leonard asked another question. "When we're in these dreams, is there anything we can do to avoid getting hurt?"

"When you're in the midst of the dream and you sense actual danger, you can remind yourself you are experiencing a dream. Tell yourself that if danger is threatening, you will leave the dream and wake up. You should tell yourself these things before you fall asleep. Do it every night before sleep and do it prior to napping. Also remind yourself that you are in control of the dream and can leave it at any time and for any reason."

"Okay." Leonard looked uncomfortable and out of sorts.

"Do you have other questions?" Simone asked the man.

"Not right now."

Libby asked, "Can dreams tell the future?"

Simone shook her head. "Not in my experience, no. Dreams may hint at things that need to be addressed in someone's waking life that may be bothering the person, or that they're struggling with, or considering, or that need to be resolved, but there is no hard and fast *future*. We influence the future by what we do today."

"We must influence what we dream about through our daily experiences, right?" Lin asked.

"Oh, yes, that's very true. Our dreams can be a time of reflection, and that reflection may be helped by considering different choices and options while we sleep."

Lin explained, "In some of my dreams, I've seen

or experienced something I didn't know about, but it had something to do with an actual thing or event from the past ... but not *my* past. How is that possible?"

"It's difficult to come up with a good answer for that so I'll tell you what many mutual dreamers think," Simone said. "You've probably heard about time being like a river that we can step into and be taken back in time by its currents. Another idea is that consciousness such as thoughts and feelings from the past may linger in the present and can be accessed or felt by some people."

Libby addressed Lin. "Would you like to share with Simone your experience when you dozed off on Viv's boat?"

Glancing down for a second, Lin took a deep breath and lifted her eyes to Simone. "I had an unusual experience the other day." She went on to tell the woman what she'd dreamt and how, when she woke, the palm of her hand was pink and red as if it had suffered a minor burn.

Simone smiled and nodded. "Earlier, Leonard asked if it's possible to get hurt in a dream. Your red palm would certainly fall into that previous question and answer. Yes, the redness could absolutely have resulted from your dream experience. It isn't uncommon at all."

"If Viv, Leonard, and I are in the same dream, can we actually touch each other?" Lin asked.

"In some cases, yes, you're able to touch a person or an object." Simone looked around at the listeners. "Have the three of you experienced the exact same dream on the same night?"

"Not exactly the same," Leonard told her. "But similar in different details."

"Okay." Simone sipped from her glass before speaking. "I'll offer you the idea of an experiment."

Viv's expression was wary as she shifted around on her chair.

"You could try falling asleep in the same place at the same time. Choose a familiar, comfortable, private place. Talk about a dream you'd like to experience together. Go over the details. Discuss how long it should last and what you want to do in the dream. Make it short and simple. An example would be … in our dream, we will be standing on the beach where we will form a circle and join hands. Lin will whisper a word in Viv's ear and she will pass it to Leonard. Then you will wake up. To prepare for the dream, sit or lie down in the same room, and go to sleep. When you wake up, you will each write down the word on a piece of paper, and then you'll share with one another. It is a simple experiment."

"I guess we could try that," Lin said with hesitation.

"Would you like to talk about the shared dreams you've been experiencing?" Simone asked.

"We talked about this before we came to the meeting," Lin spoke for the three of them. "We decided that the more general information you shared with us would be helpful, but we'd rather keep the details of our dreams to ourselves."

Simone nodded and smiled. "I understand. If I can help you with anything as you go forward, just give me a call or an email. I'm happy to answer any other questions you might come up with."

After a few more minutes of chat, Lin, Viv, and Leonard thanked the woman for her time, thanked and hugged Libby, and went outside to Viv's Jeep.

"What did you think?" Lin asked.

"It was helpful listening to her," Viv admitted. "It's so weird and hard to accept, but it made me feel better that other people experience what we do."

"It's harder for me to wrap my head around this than it was when Marguerite first showed up as a ghost." Leonard rubbed his chin. "I don't know why. Maybe because this has so many moving parts.

Marguerite was herself except in a different form. With this dream stuff ... you never know what's going to happen next. It feels unsettling. Sometimes, it feels dangerous. I don't like the unknown, and we don't know what's coming next."

"I think you nailed how we're all feeling." Lin sighed.

"It's always at the back of my mind," Leonard told them. "It's always picking at me."

"Would you like to try what Simone suggested? Do a little dream experiment like the one she gave us as an example?" Lin asked.

"It can't hurt," Viv said, and then she frowned. "Can it?"

"I guess we could give it a try," Leonard agreed. "Maybe it could speed things up so we can get this stuff over with. We need to find out the reason why Mara, the ghost, has shown up."

"I'd like to know what she wants us to do." Lin nodded. "I'd like it to be over and done."

"I have the feeling it'll all be over soon." Viv's shoulders drooped. "And I don't know if that will be a good thing ... or a bad thing."

## 22

It was a hot day for June with clear blue skies, no humidity, a calm ocean, and a good breeze that was perfect for sailing. Lin, Jeff, Viv, John, Nicky, and Queenie were in happy spirits when they boarded the boat and were soon underway following along the island's coast. They left the harbor and passed by Brant Point lighthouse where little children were frolicking in the water while adults stood, swam, or played alongside of them.

The wind blew Lin's long hair around her face and she caught it in her hand and put it into a high ponytail. She and Jeff were sitting at the bow enjoying the breeze and laughing every time water splashed up in their faces.

Nicky, with his nose sniffing the air and his small

ears flip-flopping in the breeze, sat on the cushioned bench on the aft-deck with Queenie and Viv while John handled the boat. Viv wore a yellow two-piece swimsuit and a wide-brimmed hat, and she stretched her legs out to sun herself almost dozing off from the relaxing motion of the boat moving over the sea.

John was in his glory. The ocean, boats, the sunshine, and the wind invigorated him and he wouldn't be the same person without them. Viv liked to tease that the boat came first with her husband and that she was probably a distant second, but only on good days.

As the boat approached Eel Point, John maneuvered it closer to shore and Lin and Jeff came back to join him and Viv.

"How about here? This looks good," John told them and he took care of lowering the swim deck so they could jump into the ocean for a dip and later, launch a couple of kayaks and floats into the water.

Lin and Viv were the first ones to leap into the cool water and they came up and bobbed at the surface of the clear blue-green ocean. The white sand beach of Eel Point wasn't far away and they could easily swim to shore if the mood struck them.

The guys jumped in a few minutes later and took

off swimming in an unofficial race. Nicky stood on the swim platform wagging his tail and Lin floated over to the little dog.

"Come on, Nick. You can come in with us." Lin encouraged the dog and in a few seconds, he wiggled closer to the edge and plopped in. He dog-paddled around for a while before climbing back up on the platform, shaking off the excess water from his fur, and letting out a bark before heading below to find Queenie who thought that water was only for drinking and looking at.

"His first swim of the season." Viv floated on her back. "He sure loves the water."

"He'll end up in my kayak later, for sure." Lin smiled as she thought about all the times she and Nick had shared a kayak, with her doing the paddling and the dog doing the navigating. She loved every season, but the summer months on the island were the best.

After the swim, they brought lunch up on the deck and sat around the table eating pasta salad, crunchy vegetable tacos, lobster sliders, and a green bean, tomato, and onion salad. Viv supplied the dessert of lemon-blueberry mini cheesecakes from her bookstore café and a platter of sliced fruit.

"I'm so full, I'm going to sink when I go back in

the water." Jeff stretched while sitting in his deck chair.

John brought up a pitcher of iced tea and poured glasses for everyone, and they sat around talking and soaking up the sun for another hour. After lunch, Viv and John floated in the ocean in inner tubes and Lin, Jeff, and Nicky took the two inflatable kayaks out and paddled around just off the shore. The dog wore an orange life vest and sat in the front of Jeff's kayak watching the people on the beach and the seagulls soaring overhead.

When it was time to continue the circle around the island in the boat, they packed the floats and kayaks away, toweled off, and headed off following the curve of the shoreline.

They sailed past Madaket beach, Cisco, and Miacomet beach, and as they approached Surfside, Lin reached for Jeff's hand.

"It's just about my favorite beach and now when I get near it, I start to feel some anxiety," Lin told her husband.

"It's completely understandable. There are a lot of unanswered questions so it makes you worry. Do you want to talk about the hotel? Will that help? Or do you want to avoid the subject?"

"I don't know." Lin pushed a stray strand of hair back into her ponytail.

"Turn away from the shore-view and look out at the horizon until we get to Nobadeer beach," Jeff suggested. "Then you don't have to see where the hotel used to be. Or look up and watch the jets coming in." The Nantucket airport wasn't far from Nobadeer and was a very busy place in the summer months as commercial airliners and private jets arrived and departed from the island.

"I'll watch the planes." Lin lifted her chin and pointed her eyes to the sky.

Viv came closer. "Birdwatching?" she asked her cousin.

"Sort of."

"I have a weird feeling going past Surfside," Viv whispered. "I feel all jumpy and on-edge."

"Me, too." Lin put her arm around Viv's shoulders. "Watch the planes with me. In a few minutes, we'll be off the coast of Tom Nevers and heading for 'Sconset."

"Not soon enough. I haven't felt nervous when we've been at Surfside to swim. Why this odd feeling now?"

"Another thing we need to figure out," Lin said. "This case has far more questions than answers."

"Add it to the list." Viv shook her head.

Lin eyed her. "I can smell smoke. If I glance at the dunes, I see fire flickering."

"Oh, man. Don't look that way." Viv moaned. "Is there ever any peace?"

Once they were back at the dock in the harbor, they changed clothes and were about to head into town for dinner when Lin's phone buzzed.

"It's Anton." Lin read the text. "He wants us to meet him. He has someone with him who wants to show us a drawing of the old hotel layout."

"Now?" Viv asked.

Lin nodded.

Jeff said, "Why don't you and Viv go talk to them. John and I will get a drink at the restaurant bar and wait for you to come back."

"Okay. We can do that."

"Where does he want to meet us?" Viv asked.

"At the bar by the water. Let's turn back. We must have walked right past them."

The young women kissed their husbands good-bye, and walked over to the outside bar. They saw

Anton waving at them from the patio where he was sitting on a sofa with a silver-haired man.

"This is Joseph Lightman. He's an architect. He owns a large firm in New York."

Joseph smiled and shook hands with the young women. "Anton told me you have an interest in the old hotel that was located at Surfside."

"Viv and I were both born on-island, but we knew very little about the hotel that was once there," Lin explained. "We've been looking into its history. Did you know three people died in the fire that destroyed half the hotel?"

"Anton told me as much as he knows about it. It's fascinating, isn't it? I didn't know about it either. Well, maybe I'd heard something in passing, but it made no impression on me."

The foursome talked more about island history before Joseph reached for the leather folder he had beside him and pulled out some photographs of the hotel.

"Here are some of the pictures I used to imagine the interior." Joseph spread them over the coffee table and pointed out windows, doors, and angles of the building which could hint at the layout of some of the interior rooms.

"We haven't seen some of these photos." Lin and Viv leaned forward to get better looks.

"I love the wraparound porch that was on the hotel," Viv said. "I can imagine sitting there with a cold drink watching the ocean."

Joseph agreed with her before taking a diagram from his folder. "I put this together from details gleaned from analyzing the outside of the hotel, and from this photo." He placed another picture on the table.

It was a photo of the interior of the hotel taken near the reception desk. The lobby was decorated with beautiful wallpaper, expensive rugs, comfortable furniture spread around the space, a fireplace, and an enormous crystal chandelier. The place looked elegant, but at the same time, cozy and inviting.

A woman stood at the desk with several employees.

The woman was Mara Winslow, and she was clutching the silver metal briefcase.

Joseph went over the diagram he'd put together. "I would say the owner's living quarters would be located right here. The porch has railings here that would prevent people from going to the far end of the porch. This indicates to me that this section of the hotel was private, and most likely where the owner's apartment would have been, along with some of the more expensive suites."

"So," Anton said, "we would guess that Mara, her friend, Paulette, and most likely, Lewis Whitman would be in the high-end section of the hotel."

Joseph had another diagram to overlay the one he'd already shown Lin and Viv. "This diagram shows where the damage was located. If I overlay this onto the hotel layout diagram, you can see that the fire destroyed the part of the hotel that housed the owner's apartment and the expensive suites."

"And that section is where Mara, Paulette, and Lewis lost their lives," Anton told them.

The cousins made eye contact with each other, and then turned their attention back to the layout diagrams in order to remember where certain rooms were located ... just in case they ever needed the information.

# 23

"What do you think we're supposed to do?" Viv asked, as she and Lin left the meeting with Anton and Joseph and made their way to the restaurant to meet Jeff and John. "We know who died in the fire, and we know a little bit about the hotel layout. But what are we supposed to do with what we know?"

"I really have no clue." Lin texted Jeff while she walked to tell him they were on their way.

Viv stopped suddenly and turned to her cousin with wide eyes. "Wait a second. Are we supposed to save Mara from the fire?"

Lin's heart began to race. "That *can't* be it. We can't do that. We can't go back in time and prevent her from dying in that blaze. And anyway, even if we could go back, we can't save her. It would change things about the future and we aren't going to do that. No way. Who knows what would change if Mara lived?"

"It's a terrible idea." Viv started to walk. "It better not be what Mara wants from us. It would be the first time we couldn't complete what a ghost wants us to do."

"I don't think she'd make that request," Lin said thoughtfully. "I don't think that's what she wants from us."

They went inside the restaurant, found the men, and were seated in a cozy corner of the restaurant where they explained what they'd learned from Anton's associate.

John rolled his eyes. "All of this is just too much. What does this ghost want anyway? Viv wakes up in the middle of the night from these nightmares, every single night ... sometimes, twice a night. Is there some way to stop them?"

"Viv could practice refusing to take part in the dreams," Lin suggested. "Eventually, they'd stop."

"I can't do that." Viv took a gulp from her water glass. "If I stop dreaming, I could miss something that might be important to resolving this case. And I'm not going to abandon Lin and Leonard. We're in this together, and we'll get out of it together."

Lin gave her cousin an appreciative look.

"As long as you'll be all right...." John reached for Viv's hand. "I wonder if there's buried treasure hidden in the spot where the old hotel once stood. Maybe that's what this ghost wants you to find."

Chuckles went around the table.

Lin smiled. "If we find any treasure, we're keeping it."

For the rest of the evening, the couples avoided talk of the ghost and enjoyed their dinners and being together until it was time to head home. Lin and Jeff returned to the boat with John and Viv to get Nicky, and then they strolled back to their house.

Lin stayed up late since she couldn't fall asleep and went out to the deck with the dog and sat there in the dark for a while. The case had her baffled. She knew the important threads were the fire, the metal briefcase, the shared dreams, and the three people who died in the tragedy. In all the time they'd given to the case, that was all they'd managed to come up with. What was the key to unlocking the mystery? When would the pieces come together?

Lin yawned and looked out at the shadows moving across the field from the moon lighting up the night. She was uneasy. She hoped Mara didn't want something they were unable to give her. Lin didn't know where else to look for clues. Maybe she should go back to Surfside. Maybe the hotel would appear to her again and she could glean something from it that they needed. She'd ask Viv to go with her. Lin thought about the stalled second floor renovation work that still needed to get done. She and Jeff had been so busy lately that the project had fallen by the wayside, but if they couldn't get to it anytime soon, it wouldn't matter. They really didn't need the space and it could be completed whenever it fit into their lives.

Lin stood and Nicky jumped up to go inside with her. "Let's go upstairs, Nick. I want to see Grandpa's booklet again."

The two climbed the stairs to the partially wall-boarded rooms, and Lin went to the far closet where things were still being stored. She sat on the floor and paged through the booklet until she came to the photograph of the hotel set near the dune grasses with the ocean just down the sandy hill from the building.

Lin imagined being inside. She thought of the chandelier glimmering overhead as the guests checked-in at the reception desk. Some people, wearing expensive suits and dresses, sat in the comfortable chairs near the fireplace, sipping afternoon tea and talking with one another.

She returned her gaze to the photo in the booklet and ran her finger over the picture. The windows at the far end of the hotel began to glow, and Lin dropped the booklet to the floor in surprise. Hesitantly, she leaned forward to look at the picture again.

In the black and white photo, the flames danced behind the windows. In a moment, flames shot through the roof, and then some windows blew out with a loud whooshing sound. Lin thought she heard a distant scream. A few people, looking terrified and clutching their bathrobes around them ran out of the front door and away from the hotel.

Fear flared in her chest, and then the photograph returned to what it was, a picture in an historical booklet, and nothing more.

Setting it back on the closet shelf and shutting the door, Lin saw the red light flooding in through the window and she went to look outside.

Nicky whined and wagged his tail.

Mara, glowing red, stood outside the house near the lane, staring up at the window.

Lin placed her hand on the window glass, and the ghost looked into the young woman's eyes. The red glow flared and waned, until the spirit put one hand over her heart and reached the other one up toward Lin in the window.

*I'll do what needs to be done*, Lin thought ... and then the ghost was gone.

Bright and early the next morning, Lin and Nicky got into the truck and before starting off down the road, her phone vibrated in her sweatshirt pocket.

The text was from Annabelle Lowell asking if Lin could come to see her sometime that day. When Lin replied, the woman invited her to come to the house for coffee before she went off to work, so Lin turned the truck around and headed toward Louella Lowell Martin's house.

When Lin parked and got out of the vehicle, Annabelle was waiting on the porch.

"I have my dog with me."

"I love dogs. Bring him in with you."

Nicky wiggled and squirmed when greeting the woman causing her to laugh out loud. "What a wonderful creature," she smiled and patted the brown dog. "Come into the kitchen. We can have some coffee and I'll find something to give this friendly animal."

"He really doesn't need anything. We just had breakfast."

"Nonsense. I have some baby carrots. I bet he'd like a few of those."

Lin gave Annabelle a smile. "Nicky loves carrots."

The women took seats at the table with mugs of coffee in their hands.

"How are things with Louella and your granddaughter?" Lin asked.

Annabelle shook her head. "Angela is making slow progress, but at least, it's progress. Louella has her hands full with the debt problems. Her husband sure left her a mess of trouble. She's afraid she's going to have to file for bankruptcy. I have a little savings that I gave her. I told her to get a lawyer and get some guidance. My small ranch house is paid for. Louella will move in with me, and so will Angela, when the time comes. We'll have to figure out how we'll afford the changes we'll need to make in order to accommodate the wheelchair, but we'll get to that when we need to."

Annabelle drank some of her coffee, and then gave herself a little shake. "I have some files stored on my laptop and the other night, I started to look through them to take my mind off things. I'd forgotten what I even had saved in those online folders." She looked at Lin. "Well, I found something really interesting. I don't even recall having it, but there it was. It must have gotten saved along with another file."

Excitement flooded Lin's veins. "What did you find?"

"A letter from Paulette to Mara. I printed it off for you." Annabelle went to the hutch and carried back a piece of paper. "It was written right before the fire. Paulette was working for Lewis Whitman at the time. She'd given her notice, but was finishing out her contract taking care of his son. Paulette overheard Whitman talking with a business associate. They were talking about Mara and the old hotel. Whitman said he had a great plan to swindle Mara out of a good deal of money. He had some false scheme to develop some sort of transportation from Nantucket town to the hotel, which of course, would keep Mara from losing a fortune. It's all there in the letter. It doesn't mention what the transportation thing was going to be because Whitman had lied about it to Mara. He didn't have a plan to transport tourists. It was all a lie to swindle Mara. Anyway, Paulette also wrote that she didn't think the letter would arrive in time, so she was traveling to the island to tell Mara in person."

"Wow." Lin looked at the piece of paper and read Paulette's letter. "Paulette was trying to keep Mara from making a business deal with Whitman." She lifted her eyes from the paper. "What Whitman was planning to do would probably have ruined Mara financially."

"That's right." Anger showed on Annabelle's face. "But he didn't get the chance, did he? He died in that fire. That man got what he deserved. Unfortunately, Paulette and Mara lost their lives as well."

"That explains why the three of them were at the hotel that night," Lin said.

*But what do you want me to do about it, Mara?*

# 24

Lin stopped in at Viv's bookstore-café to sit and have a coffee and a muffin before heading off to the first landscaping job of the day. Libby sat at one of the tables and waved her over. When there was a lull in the morning business, Viv sat down to join them.

"What did you think of the meeting with Simone?" Libby asked. "Was it helpful?"

"It was interesting, but weird," Viv offered. "It's so hard to understand what's going on. How does it work? How do we actually have the same dreams? What causes them?"

"Why didn't you ask Simone those questions?" Libby asked.

Viv shrugged. "At the time, I didn't think of them. My head was all a jumble. My thoughts were muddled. I had to process what she said for a few days."

"She'll come back if we want her to. Or you can arrange a call with her. What did you think, Carolin?"

"Pretty much the same things Viv thought. It was good to hear about other people's experiences with mutual dreams. It was good to hear Simone talk about it like it wasn't a big deal. The information she gave us made it seem less crazy."

"Only a *little* less crazy," Viv eyed her cousin.

"What about the experiment she talked about doing?" Libby broke off a piece of her bagel and buttered it. "Will the three of you attempt something like that?"

Lin and Viv exchanged a look.

"We've been talking about it," Viv admitted. "But we're apprehensive."

Libby's face softened. "I understand, but I think if you do a short, managed experiment, it might make you feel more in control."

Lin and Viv thought that over.

"What about Leonard?" Libby asked. "Would he be willing to do an experiment?"

Lin answered. "Leonard doesn't like any of this,

but if we decide to try a shared dream together, he'll do it."

Libby nodded. "Leonard is a sensible man, and a very good person."

With a smile, Lin said, "That's something we all agree on."

"I must get to a meeting. Do you need anything from me?"

Lin shrugged a shoulder and gave the woman a weak smile. "Your support and encouragement."

Libby looked closely at the cousins. "You have those two things from me a million times over. You call if you need me, okay?"

"We will."

Libby gave the young women warm hugs and then gathered her things and left the café.

Viv sighed. "Should we try the darned experiment and get it over with?"

"Do you feel up to it?"

"No." Viv chuckled. "But I think Libby's right. It might make us feel like we're in control."

"I'll ask Leonard when I see him today."

"John is busy this evening so if you want to get together tonight, that works for me." Viv took a sip from Lin's coffee mug.

"Jeff will be on the Vineyard with Kurt overnight tonight so it's good for me, too."

"Check with Leonard," Viv suggested. "See if he can meet up with us tonight. I'd like to get it over with."

Lin nodded.

"How are things going with Jeff and the new partnership with Kurt?" Viv asked.

"Jeff is really excited about it. He and Kurt get along great and they think the same way. It seems like it's off to a good start. They have two big jobs on the Vineyard and they're thinking they'll need to hire more help. It will either be a great financial move, or we'll lose everything."

Viv said, "I'll make sure to keep the guest room ready for you."

"Thanks." Lin finished her muffin.

Viv and Leonard arrived at Lin's house around the same time ... both looking nervous and miserable.

"We have to have a good attitude about this," Lin told them. "We have to keep positive energy around us."

"Okay," Leonard said. "How's this? I'm *positive* I'm not crazy about doing this."

"That's a downer attitude," Lin told him. "Try again."

"I'll put on a positive attitude when we're done with this experiment."

They went into the living room where Lin had set up the sofas and chairs with comfortable pillows and soft blankets.

"I thought we needed a comfortable, safe environment. I lowered the lights to make it easier to fall asleep."

Leonard sat in the easy chair and Nicky jumped up and gave him a kiss on the cheek. "Are you going to take part, too, Nick?"

The dog wagged and licked his cheek again.

"Nicky's going to keep an eye on us to make sure we're okay," Lin said.

Looking uneasy, Viv took a seat on one of the sofas. "How is this going to work?"

"We'll talk about what we want to accomplish," Lin said. "I thought we should just do the simple experiment that Simone described to us the other day. Once we fall asleep, we'll meet in our dreams, form a circle, and one of us will whisper a word into one of our ears. Then that person will pass it to the other person. Then we'll wake up and compare the word we heard. What do you think?"

"Sounds fine to me." Leonard continued to pat the dog.

"Me, too. Should we decide in advance who will say the word?" Viv questioned.

"Do either of you want to be the one who whispers the word?"

Viv looked at Leonard. "I'll do it," she said.

"Okay. Think of what word you'll use. Make it something we don't associate with you," Lin explained. "Don't choose *Queenie* or *John* or *Victus*. Make it something unexpected."

"Okay. Let me think for a minute." Viv's forehead scrunched up while she pondered what word to choose. "I have it. I'm ready."

"Whatever you do, don't forget the word and take up time trying to think of another one," Leonard said. "We want to get in and out of that dream as fast as possible."

"Are we ready to give it a try?" Lin asked.

"Let's do this thing," Leonard said.

"Yeah," Lin said. "The quicker we finish, the quicker we can have dessert. I have cheesecake."

Viv frowned. "That's my word."

"Oh. Sorry. Pick another one."

Leonard sighed.

A few moments passed before Viv said, "Okay. Let's go. I have a word in mind."

"Okay. Do you want me to put on some soft music or just have quiet?"

Viv and Leonard said in unison, "Quiet."

Lin dimmed the lights a bit more, and took a seat. They closed their eyes, and even though neither of them thought they'd fall asleep, they were deeply slumbering within ten minutes.

Lin's eye's fluttered open. It was dark and hard to see. She heard the waves crashing on the beach. She turned around, and there was the Surf Hotel, only it wasn't a vision. It was a real, solid building.

A flash of reddish-orange splashed over the roof and Lin gasped. The hotel was on fire. She spun in a circle looking for Viv or Leonard, but no one was in sight.

Lin took off running toward the front of the building, and when she reached the steps to the porch, two people came rushing outside, barefoot, and wearing bathrobes.

"Are there other people inside?" Lin shouted to them.

The couple ran past her like she didn't exist.

Flames shot out of some windows and the sound of shattering glass filled the night air. Lin looked behind her again hoping to see her friends. With her heart in her throat, she ran up the stairs and opened the front door of the hotel.

Inside was pandemonium with people screaming and frantically running about. Taking a moment to orient herself, she realized that the wing to her left was likely where Mara Winslow had her apartment. She took off her sweater and tied it around her face to cover her nose and mouth from the smoke, then she raced down the hallway.

The smoke was so heavy that Lin could barely see a thing. She used her hands to feel for the wall which she continued to follow. Screams and shouts could be heard from different parts of the hotel. The heat was intense.

Fumbling to the end of the hall, she tried to open a door, but the knob was so hot, she had to let it go. She moved further along and tried the next door, with the same result.

Lin almost turned back to the lobby, but forced herself to continue. Afraid and alone, she teared up, but when the tears fell, they dried almost instantly on her cheeks.

Feeling exhausted and confused, Lin crouched down, hoping the air closer to the floor would be less smoky. She scooted along in the crouch, feeling for the next door as she went, and stood when she found it. Grabbing the knob, she turned. It opened. She stepped into the room and followed the wall.

For a moment, the air cleared a little.

There on the floor was the woman Lin had seen in her dreams. She ran to her and felt for a pulse, but there was nothing.

"Mara?" she shouted as she shook the woman's shoulder. "Mara. Can you hear me? Can you get up?"

Then Lin stopped herself and she sat back on her heels. *I can't save her. I'm not supposed to save her.*

Coughing, she stood and glanced around the smoky room. She could hear the snaps, cracks, and explosions as fire swept through the next room.

*I need to get out of here. I need to hurry.*

Rushing to find the way out, Lin halted, and slowly turned, peering through the heavy smoke. On the floor next to Mara was the silver, metal briefcase. Hurrying back to the woman, Lin grabbed the case, and stooping low and trying to breathe shallow and quick, she made her way back to the door.

She pulled it open, but she wasn't where she thought she was. She thought she'd entered the hallway, but she was in the adjoining room to Mara's.

Disoriented and frantic, she realized she wasn't in the hall. Unable to find her way out, she panicked. Stumbling, she fell to her knees, but held tight to the case.

The heat and smoke were nearly overwhelming.

*I need to get out of here. How am I going to get out of here?*

"Viv!" she screamed. She called her cousin's name, over and over, until she began to hack and cough, and she leaned forward placing her cheek against the floor.

"Lin!"

Lin scrambled to her feet. "I'm here! I'm here, Viv. I can't get out."

Hearing something bashing against wood, Lin followed the sound until she heard a loud splintering sound.

"Lin. Where are you?" Viv screamed.

"Here. I'm coming." Lin hurried through the thick smoke toward her cousin's voice, and when she found her, tears streamed down her face as they gripped hands, and Viv led her out the way she'd come.

Behind them, part of the roof collapsed and flames shot up the walls.

Viv tugged Lin away from the inferno, and followed along the wall to the next door that led into an adjoining room. They continued like that through two more doors until the next one was locked and wouldn't budge.

Lin fell to her knees, coughing, overcome by the smoke.

Viv pounded on the door, calling Leonard's name. "Help us. We need you!"

About to give up, Viv heard Leonard calling to her and she yelled to him. In a moment, Leonard bashed his way through the door, leaned down, picked up Lin, and then, he and Viv found their way out.

Running down the front steps as the left side of the hotel collapsed with flames shooting skyward, Leonard, with Lin in his arms, ran behind Viv until they'd made it to the dunes where he lay Lin, unconscious, on the soft sand. He knelt down next to Viv, exhausted.

Leonard woke with a frantic gasp, and coughing, sat up in his chair blinking at his surroundings.

Gagging, Viv rolled into a sitting position from where she'd been lying on the sofa. She rubbed her forehead. "What happened? What's going on?" She burst into spasms of coughs.

"Viv." Leonard stood on shaky legs and went to her. "Are you okay?"

"I think so. Where's Lin?" She jumped to her feet.

They looked around the room. Lin wasn't on the other sofa.

"Where is she?" Leonard was nearly shouting, his face white, his eyes full of fear.

Nicky barked from the deck, and Leonard and Viv stared out through the glass door that led outside.

"Lin!"

Lin was lying on her side on the deck.

When they reached her, Lin started to mumble, and she moved to sit up. "Where are we?" She blinked to clear her vision. "How did I get out here?"

"Are you okay?" Leonard demanded, wrapping her in his arms.

"What happened?" she asked weakly.

Viv ran inside and came out carrying a glass of

water. She handed it to her cousin and helped her sip.

"Your hand," Lin said. "Did you burn it?"

Viv glanced at her hand, and her eyes widened. A red mark ran down the center of her hand. She looked up at Leonard. "Your hair is singed."

The man reached up to touch the side of his head, and a look of alarm washed over his face.

Squinting through the darkness, Lin asked in a whisper, "What's that?"

Viv and Leonard turned to look where she was pointing.

A silver, metal briefcase, speckled with soot, sat perched on the far end of the deck.

# 25

Lin, Viv, Leonard, and Libby walked up the little hill under the big leafy trees to a quiet spot on the edge of the older section of the cemetery on the outskirts of Boston.

"Here it is." Viv found Mara Winslow's grave marker, and the others clustered together to see it.

"It's a peaceful spot," Lin said.

Each of them lay a white rose on the grave, then they held hands and stood in a semi-circle.

Lin took a deep breath. "We did what you hoped we would. Somehow, and we don't understand any of it, we went into the fire and returned with your briefcase. The contents will be life-changing for Louella and her daughter. Your wish for them to be taken care of has come true."

"And just for the record," Leonard said. "I don't ever want to do that again."

The women smiled at the man's comment as they all went over to sit on two benches placed under a tall weeping willow tree.

When they'd found Lin outside after waking from the shared dream, Leonard gingerly picked up the metal case that sat at the end of the deck.

"Should we open it?" Viv eyed the thing like it might come to life and snap at them.

Lin said, "I don't know. We could call Anton and Libby and ask them to come over."

"Good," Leonard agreed. "Let them make the decision about it."

Libby and Anton arrived within twenty minutes and rushed into the house. When they saw the three dream-wanderers sitting quietly in the living room, Libby hurried to each one and wrapped them in a hug.

Anton's eyes got all misty. "Thank the heavens. You're all okay." He darted into the kitchen to get some antiseptic and a bandage for Viv's hand and then began to tend to her burn. He glanced at Leonard. "I can't do anything about your singed hair. Give it some time. It will grow back."

"Do you need any medical attention?" Anton asked Lin. "Are you hurt in any way?"

"Nothing's wrong with Coffin," Leonard said. "At least not physically anyway."

"I'm exhausted," Lin said weakly. "Do you have anything that can help with that?"

"Yes," he replied to Lin as he wrapped Viv's hand with gauze. "A whiskey sour. I'll make one for you in a moment. And one for me, too. I swear, your antics will be the death of me." Anton stood and headed to the kitchen once again, but this time, he made tea for those who wanted some, concocted two whiskey sours, and took a cold beer from the refrigerator for Leonard.

When they were sitting with their drinks, Libby said, "Tell us everything. Start from the beginning and don't leave anything out."

The three dreamers took turns telling the story of their adventure into the unknown.

"The dream took us to the hotel. I arrived first and the place was already engulfed. I asked someone a question, but it was like they couldn't hear or see me. I didn't exist ... at least, not to them. I ran into the hotel, figured out which way to go, and somehow ended up in Mara's apartment. The smoke was terrible. The flames were frightening. I tried to get out, but I couldn't find my way." Lin looked to her cousin. "Then Viv found me."

"When I was dreaming, I turned up in a room. I knew it was a hotel, but I didn't know it was *that* hotel ... not until I smelled the smoke and saw the fire." Viv's face blanched recalling the nightmare. "I could hear Lin calling my name. When I think back on it, if it was real-life, I wouldn't have been able to hear her because I was too far away. I rushed through the rooms, each one connected to the next by doors. It was just like the nightmares I've been having for the past weeks. My legs were like blocks of cement. I had to find Lin, but I could barely move my feet. I was determined though. I *had* to find her."

Leonard reported a similar experience to Viv's. "I woke up in the lobby. People ran all around me. There was screaming, near-hysteria. In the back of my mind, I could hear Lin and Viv calling for me." He took a deep breath. He didn't want to give many details. "I found them and carried Lin out of the hotel."

"She had the briefcase in her hand while we were shouting for Leonard. She got too weak to hold it, so I picked it up," Viv said. "The handle is what burned my skin."

"When we got to the dunes, I rested Lin on the

ground. The next thing we knew, Viv and I were back here in the living room."

Viv added, "We realized Lin wasn't with us. Nicky saw her out on the deck. We were all disoriented for a while, trying to make sense of what happened."

"We spotted the briefcase," Leonard said. "Then we called you."

"You haven't opened it?" Anton questioned.

All three shook their heads.

"Should we?" Viv asked.

Anton tilted his head. "Well, since a ghost appeared, caused you to have shared dreams, managed to get you into a long-ago hotel in the middle of a fire, and you return to real life with a metal briefcase, then I'd say the whole point of this adventure was to get at what's inside that thing. Of course, we should open it."

Lin managed a smile. "Since you put it that way...."

"Is it locked?" Libby asked.

"There's one way to find out." In the middle of the room, Anton knelt beside the case and inspected the lock. "It doesn't seem to be locked." He looked from Lin to Viv to Leonard. "Would either of you like to do the honors?"

They answered together, "No."

Without another word, Anton laid the case on its side, flicked the latch, and opened it. He lifted a black velvet jewelry container to see strands of pearls, diamond rings and necklaces, and emerald earrings. He next removed a large dark blue leather case and when he opened it, everyone's eyes widened. The holder was stuffed full of money. He set it on the floor, and the last thing he took out of the briefcase was a black leather folder. Anton stared at the contents. "Stock certificates. Lots of them. From many different companies." He read some of the company names. "Oh, my. These are … oh, gosh, there must be a fortune right here in these certificates." He held some of them up so the others could see.

Lin rested her head on the sofa back. "A fortune. Just what Louella needs."

Viv's eyes went wide. "That was the reason. That's what Mara wanted. She needed us to go back into the hotel and retrieve that briefcase because the contents would take care of Annabelle, Louella, and Angela for the rest of their lives."

"She knew her descendants were headed for financial ruin," Libby said.

"Mara needed to save them," Lin smiled.

"But where was the briefcase all this time since the fire?" Anton asked with a confused expression. "Clearly, it was never found after the fire."

"Who knows?" Lin said. "We don't know where the case has been all this time and we don't know who set the hotel fire. We don't even know if someone *did* set it. It may have happened from some other cause. And we have no idea how these shared dreams work. We have to accept that there are some things in the world we'll never understand. I'd like to know the answers to all of these questions, but we had one aim ... to bring back that briefcase. And we did it. We accomplished what Mara needed us to do. The rest of it doesn't matter. We *did* what mattered. We helped Mara help her family. That's the most important thing of all."

While they sat under the tree in the cemetery, Libby got a call. "It's Anton." After listening to what he had to say, she spoke with him for a few minutes and then ended the call. She looked at the three people with her, an expression of disbelief on her face.

"What did Anton want?" Lin asked.

Libby took a deep breath. "There's a preliminary

estimate for the worth of the things from that briefcase."

They waited, and when she didn't say anything, Viv said, "Well, tell us, for Pete's sake."

"Ten." Libby paused.

"Ten what?" Lin asked.

"Ten million dollars."

Everyone was stunned into silence for a few seconds, and then they whooped and hollered with joy.

"Ten million?" Viv's mouth dropped open. "Oh, my gosh. Wait. Is there anything that was left behind from *our* ancestors like that?" She laughed. "We need to look into this. Maybe we can share-dream our way to our own fortune."

They chattered about the amazing good luck for a while longer and then Viv told them it was time to leave to go into the city to meet Jeff, John, and Heather at the restaurant where they were having dinner together that night.

As they got up to leave, Libby said, "Anton is working with a lawyer who will handle the transfer of the money, jewelry, and stocks to Annabelle and Louella. Tomorrow they're going to speak with the women about the inheritance. Anton is concocting a tale to tell them about how the briefcase came into his possession."

"I can't wait to hear what he comes up with," Lin grinned.

"It better be a doozy," Leonard told them.

At the bottom of the hill, Lin was surrounded by the familiar sensation of being enveloped with chilly air. She stopped and looked back up the hill to see Mara Winslow smiling down at them. Mara placed her hand over her heart, nodded, and then disappeared.

"What is it?" Viv put her hand on her cousin's arm.

"Mara." Lin's heart filled with warmth. "She came to tell us thank you."

Lin and Jeff biked to the top of the hill and turned into the field that led to the oldest house on the island.

"I love this place." Lin let her eyes wander over the beautiful setting of the meadow, the antique house, the trees.

She and Jeff walked their bikes along the path,

and took a seat on a bench to share a granola bar and some water.

"It's nice to have that case over and done with," Jeff handed the container of water to his wife. "It sure was a weird one."

Lin nodded. "At least it had a happy ending. Annabelle and Louella will be set for life, and they have the money to give Angela the very best surgeons and aftercare. Her prognosis is looking up Anton told me. Angela will have a few minor physical limitations, but over time, she'll make a good recovery."

"That's excellent news. Now you can enjoy a well-deserved break from ghosts and mysteries."

Lin smiled as something caught her eye in one of the windows of the old house. "Is the house open for tourists and visitors already? I thought it opened later today."

"I don't think it's open. Why do you think so?"

"Huh. I thought I saw someone pass by the window. It must have been the sunlight flickering over the glass."

"Oh." Jeff took a look at the house. "Maybe we'd better get on with our bike ride. We never know when something's going to interrupt our plans."

Lin chuckled and stood. "Well, in case something

interrupts us soon...." She took a step closer to Jeff, put her arms around his waist, and kissed him.

"What was that for?" Jeff grinned.

"Because my husband is the best guy in the world, that's why."

They got back onto their bikes, and as they started away to the road, Lin glanced over her shoulder to take one more look at the house.

*Hmm.*

---

I hope you enjoyed *The Haunted Hotel*! The next book in the series, *The Haunted Dwelling*, can be found here:

viewbook.at/TheHauntedDwelling

## THANK YOU FOR READING!

Books by J.A. WHITING can be found here:
www.amazon.com/author/jawhiting

To hear about new books and book sales, please sign up for my mailing list at:
www.jawhiting.com

Your email will never be sold, shared, or spammed.

If you enjoyed the book, please consider leaving a review. A few words are all that's needed. It would be very much appreciated.

## BOOKS BY J. A. WHITING

SWEET COVE PARANORMAL COZY MYSTERIES

LIN COFFIN PARANORMAL COZY MYSTERIES

CLAIRE ROLLINS PARANORMAL COZY MYSTERIES

MURDER POSSE PARANORMAL COZY MYSTERIES

PAXTON PARK PARANORMAL COZY MYSTERIES

ELLA DANIELS WITCH COZY MYSTERIES

SEEING COLORS PARANORMAL COZY MYSTERIES

OLIVIA MILLER MYSTERIES (not cozy)

SWEET ROMANCES by JENA WINTER

COZY BOX SETS

# BOOKS BY J.A. WHITING & NELL MCCARTHY

## BOOKS BY J.A. WHITING & ARIEL SLICK

GOOD HARBOR WITCHES PARANORMAL COZY MYSTERIES

## BOOKS BY J.A. WHITING & AMANDA DIAMOND

PEACHTREE POINT COZY MYSTERIES

DIGGING UP SECRETS PARANORMAL COZY MYSTERIES

# BOOKS BY J.A. WHITING & MAY STENMARK

MAGICAL SLEUTH PARANORMAL WOMEN'S FICTION COZY MYSTERIES

HALF MOON PARANORMAL MYSTERIES

## VISIT US

www.jawhiting.com

www.bookbub.com/authors/j-a-whiting

www.amazon.com/author/jawhiting

www.facebook.com/jawhitingauthor

www.bingebooks.com/author/ja-whiting

J. A. Whiting Books

Printed in Great Britain
by Amazon

42075868R00158